THE TOUCH OF THE ICE

Nicholas Walker was born in the West Midlands. He studied law for a time and has worked in a variety of jobs, including banking, running clubs, hotels and two pubs. At the age of twenty-one he became the youngest licensee in Britain, running a pub in Wales. He went on to own a large specialist seafood restaurant in the holiday town of Penzance.

His interests are very wide and include such sports as cycling (he once did a sponsored cycle ride from John O'Groats to Lands End), parachute jumping, rock climbing and ice skating. Nicholas holds a 3rd Dan in karate and for the last five years has run his own martial arts organization.

He is now a part-time science teacher as well as a full-time author. Besides writing articles for magazines and newspapers, his other works for children include *Crackling Ice* and *Skating on the Edge*, also available in Piper, and a series of sports novels published by Blackie. Nicholas lives in Essex and has two children.

Also available by Nicholas Walker in Piper

CRACKLING ICE
SKATING ON THE EDGE

Nicholas Walker

The Touch
of the Ice

A Piper Original
PAN MACMILLAN
CHILDREN'S BOOKS

First published 1993 by Pan Macmillan Children's Books

a division of Pan Macmillan Publishers Limited
Cavaye Place London SW10 9PG
and Basingstoke

Associated companies throughout the world

ISBN 0 330 32907 3

1 3 5 7 9 8 6 4 2

A CIP catalogue record for this book is available from
the British Library

Typeset by CentraCet Limited, Cambridge
Printed and bound in Great Britain by
Cox & Wyman Ltd, Reading, Berkshire

For Elizabeth

CONTENTS

1

CLOAK AND DAGGER

The rink was packed with cheering fans. Even in the massive Coliseum every seat was taken. The ice was scattered with flowers, so much so that the skaters had to go warily.

In the middle of the ice a podium had been set up and already two couples occupied second and third places. The MC was waiting for silence but he could have waited all night so in the end he had to resort to shouting into the microphone:

'And the Senior Ice Dance champions are Alex Barnes and Samantha Stephens!' But his final words were lost in the huge roar that went up as the crowd showed their appreciation for the winners from the home rink. They came forward and carefully stepped up into the middle position on the podium.

Right in the back row, Sir Robert Sinclair, president of the National Ice Skating Association, leaned closer to Liz Pope so she could hear him.

'Well, that was a foregone conclusion,' he said.

Liz shook her head. 'It's never a foregone conclusion,

1

especially with the free dances those two put on – they're too dangerous,' she said. 'And bear in mind that Melodie Saxon and Lester Carmichael aren't here.'

'Hm, yes, where are they?' asked Sir Robert.

'Off training in Florida somewhere,' said Liz, and her voice was disapproving.

'It might not have made any difference,' said Sir Robert. 'Your two have come a long way in a very short time.'

'They're not my two,' said Liz. 'They just come to my dance class. I'm not their trainer.'

'So I understand,' said Sir Robert. 'It's remarkable that they have come this far without professional help – oh, look, they're getting the cup.' He broke off to join in the applause as Alex held the cup high in the air. When it died down Sir Robert turned to find Liz eyeing him sardonically.

'Is that what this is all about?' she asked.

'How do you mean?'

'The reason you're here. At a minor competition like this.'

'That's not fair, Mrs Pope. I try to make every competition,' he said. 'We like to keep an eye on any prospective talent.' He turned in his seat to face her, getting down to business at last. 'Though perhaps you can tell me why they haven't approached a trainer. Or, rather, why one hasn't approached them.'

Liz sighed. 'Alex can't afford one,' she said. 'His father was made redundant last year and Alex has to finance his skating himself.'

'But surely *her* father's some big-name accountant, isn't he?' asked Sir Robert.

'Yes, he's the Stephens in Parslow, Stephens and Kerr, you've probably heard of them, and by all accounts' – she smiled briefly at the unintended pun – 'he's very well off.'

'Doesn't he approve of Samantha skating then?'

'Mr Stephens approves of anything his daughter wishes him to,' said Liz. 'No, he's very generous, but that's the whole point. Samantha won't let him pay for everything because it would make Alex feel bad.'

'If they want to really compete I'm not sure they can afford sentiments like that,' grunted Sir Robert.

'Yes, but you don't understand the relationship, Sir Robert,' said Liz. 'Samantha's got all the drive, especially when it comes to the skating. But Alex is no doormat, and he's still young enough to be worried about his macho image; if he got the idea he was scrounging off Samantha he'd walk away.'

'Money doesn't have to be a problem,' said Sir Robert. He leaned back in his seat. 'I'd like them to meet someone afterwards.'

Back on the ice Samantha gave Alex's hand a secret squeeze. His squeeze back was automatic. He was concentrating more on the audience, searching for his friend, Toby. Even Toby's huge voice had been stilled by the uproar.

'If he's slipped off to the hot-dog stand . . .' Alex muttered.

'What?' Samantha managed to make herself heard as the noise died down a bit.

'Never mind.' He gave her a smile. 'What was all that business in the last part of the fight? You're supposed to face me, not the crowd!'

3

'I split my costume,' she said. 'That last jump, I felt it go.'

'Where?'

'Never mind.'

'Ah.' Alex grinned. 'It doesn't matter, we've finished with the Cloak and Dagger free now, haven't we?'

'Oh, yes, there isn't anybody left in the entire world who hasn't seen it by this time,' said Samantha. 'Come on, I think we can make a break for it now, they must be sick of cheering.'

'Yes, but I'm not sick of hearing them cheer,' he said. 'Just because it's the first time they've had a winner from here.' He stepped off the podium and handed her back down onto the ice. Carefully she kept her back to him so she was hidden from the crowd by the huge cloak he was wearing.

'Slowly now,' she hissed, 'and keep close behind.'

When Liz came into the anteroom Samantha was sitting on a bench, leaning back against the wall, her eyes closed. Her left hand was clasped firmly around the base of a large silver cup on the seat beside her. She looked exhausted. At the sound of Liz's footsteps she opened one eye and regarded her for a moment. Liz went over and gave her a hug:

'Well done,' she said quietly.

'Did you see the split in my dress?' Samantha demanded.

'You split it?'

'Comprehensively!'

'You couldn't see it from the auditorium.'

'That's all right then.' Samantha shut her eyes again.

4

'Where's Alex?'

'Lost his shoes, or his shirt — something anyway,' said Samantha.

'I'm here,' said Alex, coming through the door. He was wearing one battered trainer and one football boot. 'Look at this!' — he held up his foot with the boot on — 'How the hell can anybody go off wearing one trainer?'

Samantha regarded him levelly through one eye. 'I like it,' she said, 'very swish.'

Liz sighed. 'You had to go and lose it tonight, didn't you?' she said. 'Just when I want you to meet somebody.'

'Oh, save me,' groaned Samantha. 'Listen, Liz, I'm knackered.'

'Don't be,' said Liz. 'Look, I've had the president of NISA sniffing around. He's got his eye on you.' Samantha sat up and condescended to open both eyes.

'Wow, big time,' she said.

Alex looked up from his preoccupation with his feet. 'What's he want?' he asked.

'He wants you to have a trainer,' said Liz.

'Oh, not again,' sighed Samantha.

'We've got a trainer — you,' said Alex.

'No you haven't,' said Liz. 'I just help out occasionally. He means a proper, professional trainer!'

'We don't want a proper, professional trainer,' said Samantha.

'Yes, you do!' said Liz earnestly. 'Look, believe me, I'll be sorry to lose you but you're going too high for me nowadays. I'm just a small-time ice-dance teacher.'

Alex came over and gave her a hug. 'Don't put yourself down, we've done all right with you.'

'You've done all right by yourselves,' said Liz.

'Liz, listen, we can't afford a professional trainer, you know that,' said Samantha.

'I know, NISA knows, everybody knows,' said Liz. 'The money's being handled, it isn't going to cost you anything.'

'Why?' demanded Alex.

'Trainers do help out like that,' said Liz. 'At least come and meet him.'

'He can't be any good if he's free,' said Samantha.

'He's one of the best,' said Liz. 'Look, I'll tell you straight, if the president of NISA says you're to have a trainer then I strongly recommend you listen to him – he's got enormous power.'

Samantha sighed and got to her feet. 'I'm not promising to be nice to him,' she said.

'What's new about that? You're never nice to anybody,' said Alex. 'What's his name, Liz?'

'Walt,' said Liz. 'Walt Danvers.'

Walt Danvers was nearly all teeth. The great smile seemed to stretch right around his head. He was also American, and he gushed. These were the four first impressions that hit Alex when Liz introduced them and he knew that at least three out of the four would rub Samantha up the wrong way.

'Well, well, well, here we are at last,' said Walt, rubbing his hands together enthusiastically. 'I've been wanting to meet you two all night long.'

'Er, yes,' said Alex, taken aback. He held out his hand. 'How do you do, sir?'

'Not sir! Walt!' he said, taking Alex's outstretched hand in both of his and squeezing it hard. He turned to

Samantha who had put her hands safely out of harm's way behind her back.

'And you, little lady, don't be shy!' said Walt, adding yet another reason to the four. Alex hurriedly interrupted before he was treated to one of Samantha's searing retorts.

'Liz said something about you training us,' he said.

'Yes, I've been watching you skate tonight. I'm sure we can work well together,' he said. 'Sir Robert has explained that you're in dire need of a trainer.'

'Has he?' said Samantha coldly.

'Now, don't you worry, little lady. I'm sure Mrs Pope here has explained that it's not going to cost you a single cent – or should I say a single penny?' He laughed and politely Alex laughed with him.

'We're most grateful,' said Alex. 'Aren't we, Samantha?' Samantha turned an incredulous stare on him. He hit her with one of his elbows.

'Er . . . Yeah,' she managed, and even the most generous person in the whole world couldn't have said she sounded grateful.

Walt came forward and draped an arm around each of their shoulders.

'I'm looking forward to a good long relationship, and a successful one,' he said.

'So are we,' said Alex.

'Absolutely,' said Samantha. She extricated herself from his arm by kneeling down and pretending to adjust her shoe. Walt's eyes followed her then switched to Alex. He leaned closer.

'Tell me something, son,' he said conversationally, 'you always wear footwear like that, do you?'

2

THE TOUCH OF
THE ICE

When Alex came out of the changing room Samantha was waiting for him. She was leaning against the corridor wall, half asleep. It was six-thirty the following Tuesday morning and they had been up since five.

'You look enthusiastic,' he said.

'Get stuffed!' she said charmingly. 'Why did I have to take up a sport with such bloody awful hours? I mean, this is ridiculous. No one's up at this time of the morning.'

'I expect any sport at a high level gets pretty unsociable,' said Alex. 'Come on, you'll soon wake up when we're on the ice.'

'Do we really have to?' she grumbled, unlike the usual enthusiastic Samantha.

'Look, it's the only time Walt had free,' said Alex. 'After all, it's only an hour earlier than we're used to.'

'If we must,' she sighed. 'Let's go and find Wart.'

'Give the poor bloke a chance,' said Alex. 'At least with him as our trainer we get use of the small rink.'

The Coliseum had two rinks – one full size, the smaller one alongside kept exclusively for the trainers, uncluttered

8

by the general public. It had a full length mirror the whole width of the ice. The huge Coliseum sports complex wasn't really Samantha and Alex's home rink but they had started skating there twice a week the previous year when Samantha had been sent away to school and they had to skate in secret.

Walt was already with another skater, a girl of about seventeen. He acknowledged Alex and Samantha, then left them alone for ten minutes, concentrating on his other pupil. Alex fidgeted while Samantha stretched. After a few minutes she stood up again, easing her leg muscles.

'Let's go on the big rink,' she suggested.

'He'll be finished in a minute!'

'We could get warmed up.'

'We can't, Samantha, it'd look rude.'

'Rude? Oh, yes, rude,' said Samantha sliding back effortlessly into side splits. 'You mean like dragging us out of bed at five o'clock in the morning, then keeping us hanging around?'

Alex avoided answering. At last the girl came off the ice and stood chatting casually for another five minutes. When she had gone Walt seemed very pleased to see them, his huge smile as wide as ever.

'Hi, you two,' he said enthusiastically. 'Sorry to keep you but Maxine's always late for her skating lesson.'

'Oh, that's what she was doing, was it?' said Samantha. 'I did wonder.'

Walt grinned. 'Yes, I know, but her mother pays good money.' He rubbed his hands together. 'Now, how about a bit of a warm up, then a quick run through your compulsories?'

'Which ones?' Alex asked. 'All of them?'

'Ah, just choose a couple, anything you like,' said Walt. At last they stepped out onto the ice. Normally, the very touch of the ice sent a frisson through them but today things seemed all wrong. They skated around getting warmed up, extemporizing, trying out moves, like a jazz musician experimenting with a theme.

'Archery,' she said mysteriously.

'Eh?'

'I bet archers don't get up at this time of the morning,' she said. 'I'd have liked to be an archer. You can always find a target, can't you?' She glanced ringside where Walt was drinking something from a Thermos flask.

'We're not paying him, Samantha,' said Alex seriously. 'I'm sure plenty of skaters would be only too willing to take our place.' Samantha didn't answer; without a word she went straight into the waltz, Alex matching her step for step with that eerie communication only perfect partners achieve. They didn't talk, both cross with the other, their skating suffering. After only ten minutes a whistle blast drew them back to the edge of the ice.

'Sorry, Walt, we've not got it together yet this morning,' said Alex.

'Eh? No, you were fine,' said Walt. 'Just don't go mad, get your breath back.'

'We haven't lost it yet,' said Samantha coldly.

'You should enjoy your skating,' said Walt. 'You don't have to skate like it was a competition every time you're on the ice.'

'You really think we'd be here at this time of morning if we didn't enjoy skating?' said Alex.

10

'And it's not worth doing if we're not going to do it the best we can,' snapped Samantha.

Walt laughed. 'Yes, I had heard you were a bit intense, little lady,' he said. Samantha's eyes went blank. Walt didn't seem to notice. 'Now, we've got to spend a lot of time on your compulsories,' he went on. 'They're your weakest point, of course.'

'So everyone keeps telling us,' said Alex.

'Mm, Samantha here is not really strong enough to cut the really deep edges you need,' said Walt. He put his arm around her shoulders. 'Don't worry, it'll come.'

Samantha swallowed. 'That'll be nice,' she said, through her teeth.

'We've got to put together a new free dance before we go for any more competitions,' said Alex.

'Oh, we'll soon throw something together,' said Walt. 'The great thing is to get ahead in the compulsories, give the judges something to look at. The free will come naturally from a good sound knowledge of the basics.'

'The free dance is our strength,' said Samantha. 'We can't go on using the same one.'

'You mean the Cloak thing?' said Walt. 'Oh, no, that's not the sort of thing you need at this level – much too gimmicky.'

Alex saw Samantha's face contort and knew that she'd been patient long enough and was about to say something really rude. He stepped in hurriedly.

'It went down really well, Walt,' he said. 'It's rather our style, that sort of thing. Samantha's brilliant at putting a free dance together.'

'No, no, like I said, it was all right for these minor

11

competitions – nice and flashy,' said Walt. 'But, that's not the fashion now, it's all long flowing movements, more along classical lines.' He gave them both his brilliant smile. 'Don't worry about it, little lady, I'll soon put something together for you.'

3

ALEX SPOILS
A TRIFLE

Toby very gently eased the last strawberry into place and
stood back to admire his handiwork.

'That one's not straight,' said a voice. He turned around
surprised, to find Alex grinning at him.

'What are you doing here?' Toby demanded.

'I hope I've come for lunch,' said Alex. 'I don't mind
having the bit with the crooked strawberry.'

Toby sighed. 'It's like that to show it's homemade. It's
called artistic licence.'

'Oh,' said Alex respectfully. 'What is it anyway?'

'Mille-feuille.'

'Eh? Mill flowers?'

Toby sighed again. 'A kind of vanilla slice to you.' He
picked up a knife, gently cut a piece and handed it to his
friend.

'Ta – doesn't it matter?' said Alex.

'No, I was just having a bit of a practice.'

'Don't you have teachers or tutors or anything?' asked
Alex, gesturing around the long kitchen where only a
handful of other students were working.

13

'Teachers? At the Stella Leigh College of Catering!' said Toby horrified. 'You mean resident chefs! Yes, but this is just a free.'

Alex smiled but he knew Toby was only half joking. His friend had done exceptionally well to be one of the twenty students accepted each year into the internationally acclaimed catering college.

'How did you get in? There are people everywhere,' said Toby.

'I just walked, you only have to look confident—' Alex broke off as a well-built boy of about eighteen pushed between them.

'Move yourself, barrel!' the boy said to Toby. He glared at Alex. 'And your pretty girlfriend here!' He barged Alex out of the way and went across to the other side of the kitchen. Alex watched him go, a thoughtful look on his face.

'Who's Mr Personality?' he asked, levelly.

'Oh, Martin,' said Toby. 'You know we all have a cross to bear? Well, he's mine – shouldn't you be in college?'

Alex shrugged. 'I didn't feel like it,' he admitted.

'You're supposed to be taking A levels, aren't you?' said Toby with a shudder. 'What was it? Maths, physics and chemistry?'

'Well, I'm not missing much today,' said Alex. Then he gave a grin. 'Only maths, physics and chemistry.'

'Where's Sammy?' Toby asked. Samantha was at the same sixth-form college as Alex retaking her GCSEs. Most of her grades had been appalling, not surprisingly, as they weren't in ice dancing.

'Dunno, working I hope, her mum'll go mad if she

14

doesn't do better this year,' said Alex. 'Look, Toby, do you feel like going out tonight?'

'What?' Toby started in surprise. 'Alex, it's Thursday – skating! Remember?'

'Not for the moment; our new trainer says we're skating too much,' said Alex. 'We're only supposed to do two mornings and three nights a week. He says we'll overtrain otherwise – whatever that means.'

'You used to skate twice a day!'

'Yeah, but apparently that's the way you get stress fractures,' said Alex. 'And we're supposed to give our muscles time to relax after each session, so once a day is more than enough.'

'Wow, I bet Sammy loves that,' said Toby. 'Why aren't you going out with her?'

Alex avoided his eyes. 'Can I have another piece of that mill flowers stuff?'

Toby handed him a piece on the end of the knife. 'Aren't you in training?'

'Walt says I can afford to put on a few pounds. I should be able to lift Samantha better if I do.'

'Walt?'

'Our trainer,' said Alex.

'Walt,' Toby repeated. 'Nobody's called Walt – unless they make cartoons.'

'He's American,' said Alex as though that explained it. 'I thought we could have a night out. We haven't been out for ages.'

'Fine.' Toby regarded Alex for a long moment. 'Oh, I get it, Sammy's going to the rink and you're not. You fallen out?'

'Not really, we just get a bit sick of each other now and then.' Alex paused. 'I don't know. If you were given — given, mind you — a trainer, one of the best in the world, you'd listen to him. Am I right?'

'Absolutely.'

'He's had two World champions, Toby.'

'I'm not arguing with you.'

'If one of your resident cooks—'

'Chefs,' put in Toby.

'Sorry, chefs,' said Alex. 'Anyway, if one of your resident chefs told you that something you were doing was wrong, you'd take his advice, wouldn't you?'

'Sure,' said Toby. He sighed. 'Look, Alex, you really want my opinion?'

'No — I really want you to agree with me,' said Alex, honestly.

Toby grinned. 'Well, I do in a way. I once told you we were both artists, remember?' he said. 'As a fellow artist I'd listen to criticism from an expert but in the end I'd still do what my heart was telling me.'

'Fine, that's what I'm doing,' said Alex crossly. 'A year ago, when we had all that trouble, we only managed to get in a skating session twice a week, and we did all right then!'

'No need to get cross with me,' said Toby. 'It's not me that's going skating without you.'

'Leave it out, Toby,' said Alex. 'About tonight — are you on?'

'Yeah, sure. I was going to a football match but as you don't like football I expect we're not now.'

'Oh, I knew it would have to be a football match or a

cooking competition,' said Alex. 'Don't you have any other interests?'

Toby thought for a moment, then shook his head. 'No,' he replied, unembarrassed.

'Whatever happened to that girl? What's her name?'

'Hilary?' supplied Toby. 'Actually it's a bit of a tragic story.'

'What happened?' asked Alex, concerned.

'You know how clever she was? How good she was at school?'

'Yeah?'

'Well, she's thrown it all away! Just when she had her pasta perfect she goes and drops Home Economics.' Toby looked sad. 'She's ended up trying for a place at Oxford, reading law.'

Alex sighed. 'OK, Toby,' he said, 'football will be fine.'

'Oh,' Toby said, surprised. 'You sure?'

'I said so, didn't I?' said Alex, sliding off the table where he had parked himself. 'I'll come round to your place around six-thirty.'

'OK,' said Toby, but he was already speaking to Alex's back. Toby shook his head; his friend was definitely in an iffy mood. He watched as Alex made his way over to where Martin was decorating a trifle with a circle of cherries. Alex gripped him firmly by the neck and jammed his face into the dish. He held the struggling figure for a full ten seconds before letting him up for air. Then, after delivering a few terse remarks, he left the cream-bespattered Martin for dead.

Yes, thought Toby, Alex was definitely in an iffy mood.

*

17

That same night, while Alex stood shivering on a touch line masking a yawn, Samantha was trying to get rid of her bad mood by skating furiously. The ice was packed but the centre was relatively clear and Samantha's instincts took her round any intruder without conscious thought. She skirted a girl at breakneck speed then recognized who it was and let her momentum take her in a complete circle and die away in a shower of ice.

'Hello, Samantha,' said Monica, looking nervous.

'Where were you last Saturday?' Samantha demanded.

'I'm sorry, I was invited to a tennis party,' said Monica.

'A tennis party?' Samantha glared at the younger girl whom she helped to train. 'You missed skating for a game of tennis?'

'Well, yes, I didn't think it would matter for *one* Saturday,' said Monica. 'And there was this boy—'

'It does matter!' said Samantha savagely. 'Skating comes first! Always first!' Monica looked upset. Samantha took a deep breath to calm herself. Monica wasn't nearly as tough as she was and Samantha had reduced her to tears on more than one occasion. 'Listen, I'm sorry I sounded off,' she said more gently, 'but if you're going to get anywhere you never let anything or anybody get in the way of a practice – understand?'

'Yes, sorry.'

'OK. Now, have you had a word with your parents about skating a couple of mornings a week?'

'They went up the wall,' said Monica. 'My dad says I'm doing too much as it is.'

'Same old problem,' sighed Samantha. 'OK, let's get

your Preliminary medal out of the way, then you can start working on them again – yes?'

'OK.'

'Right, I'll take you through your medal dances right now to try and make up for Saturday.'

The two girls skated off around the rink.

4

SOMEONE
TO HOLD ON TO

On Friday evenings Alex and Samantha always skated late. There was an ice hockey match on first, then the ice had to be resurfaced, so it was usually nine o'clock before the public was admitted.

Alex laced up his skates and made his way down onto the ice. He was feeling nervous about meeting Samantha. They hadn't seen each other since Wednesday.

Samantha was in the middle, skating the same move again and again, when Alex materialized at her side.

'Hi,' he said.

'Oh, hi,' she said neutrally, meeting his eyes.

'Been here long?'

'No,' she said, but he knew she was lying because there were circles cut everywhere in the centre of the rink. 'Your tutor was asking where you were at college.'

'I felt like some time off,' said Alex. 'Shall we do a bit of work?'

'If you like.' He took her in his arms and they went round the ice, gently at first, then throwing themselves more into it as he warmed up. But it wasn't a successful session. There was still a distance between them caused by their disagreement over Walt. They concentrated on the compulsories and went through them all. It was practice of a kind but it wasn't taking them any further.

When they met outside the rink after the session they were still half wary of one another. They'd reached the end of Samantha's road before Alex at last broached the subject they were both thinking about.

'You skated last night then, did you?'

'I said I was going to.'

'How did you get on?'

'Oh, fine, just great.' The words were bitter.

'You going to tell Walt?'

'If he asks, I'm not afraid of him knowing,' said Samantha.

'Even though he's expressly asked us not to?' said Alex, becoming slightly more heated.

'He doesn't own me, Alex,' she said mildly.

'He doesn't own me either! I just think he's worth listening to,' said Alex. 'What did you work on?'

'Our new free.'

'Oh, Samantha!' Alex said.

'What does that mean?' she demanded. Alex stopped walking and faced her.

'It means that Walt says he's going to work on our free dance with us,' said Alex.

'You mean you'd rather he did it than me?'

'I didn't say that! Obviously we'll all work on it together.' Alex ran his fingers through his hair. 'Look, he

21

must know the kind of things the judges are looking for – if we stay with him we could be in the British championships next year!'

'If we get into the British championships then, it'll be because we deserve it!' snapped Samantha.

'Even you don't believe that,' said Alex. 'You have to get yourself known!'

'I thought we were doing OK on that score,' said Samantha.

'Yes, but we can do better,' said Alex. 'Look, he's got to know his job, he's had two World champions. If he says we're training too much, then he must be right.' She shook her head. This annoyed Alex more than ever.

'He explained it to you, didn't he, genius? If your muscles don't get time to relax between sessions then you can't progress – or weren't you listening?' he said crossly. 'I've been talking to the other skaters in Liz's dance class. Nobody works anything like as hard as we do – none of them goes for runs, or cycle rides, or spends every night doing press ups!'

'And none of them is doing as well as we are . . . *were*!' she snapped back, finally jerked out of her complacency. 'You listen to me, Alex Barnes, I was at dance school for over ten years—'

'Oh, here we go! The gospel according to the Tracy Powell School of Dance!'

'Yes, where they know more about dance and exercise and muscles than any idiot American who just happened to get hold of a couple of World champions a hundred years or so ago—' She broke off, then, 'Oh, forget it, you're not even listening.'

22

'I hear you talking,' he said. 'Look Samantha—'

'Oh, just go away!' she said. 'You'll always be a loser, Alex Barnes!' She ran off up the road. Alex watched her go but didn't run after her.

Samantha lay on her bed staring at the ceiling. She had heard her parents come up hours before but hadn't even attempted to shut her eyes.

Suddenly, she came bolt upright. A stone had bounced off her window. She fought to bring her breathing back under control before she glanced out of the window. Then she quickly slipped into her track suit, opened her window, and climbed into the tree that grew up the side of the house. She slid down with the ease of the athlete that she was and landed right in his arms. They stood hugging each other tightly but not speaking for nearly two minutes. Finally he spoke.

'Hey, you're shaking.'

'It's the cold,' she said. Alex nodded, though the night was warm. 'I'm sorry about calling you a loser,' she said into his shoulder.

'That's all right. You want to hear what I called you,' he said. 'Anyway, if you thought I was a loser you would have dumped me years ago.'

'I can't do it without you, Alex. I need someone to hold on to.'

'On the ice, you mean?'

'That as well,' she said. 'That's why I'm such a pain in the ass!'

'I'm glad you realize it,' he grinned. She pushed him away, not angrily, but so she could talk better.

'Well, you can be such an airhead at times!'

'Thanks.'

'Well, you can be!' There was a pause before she tried again. 'Look, I know I'm spoilt, my parents have always spoilt me. I'm used to getting my own way – and I sulk when I don't! But this time I'm right!'

'You think you are.'

'I know I am,' she said crossly. Then added in a much quieter voice, 'Sorry.'

'Look, Samantha, all I'm asking you to do is consider that you might be wrong just this once – work with Walt, not against him.'

'It's just that . . .' She broke off avoiding his eyes. 'I miss you on the ice, Alex.'

'I miss you as well. Do you really think I wanted to go and watch a bunch of idiots kick a ball about in a muddy field?'

'No, of course not.' She put her arms around him again. 'I don't want to fall out with you any more.'

'You mean it affects our skating?' Alex grinned.

'You know what I mean.' She stood on tiptoe and kissed him, a nice kiss. 'Don't worry, I'll wait for you,' she said.

'What do you mean? Wait for me?' he demanded.

'I mean this business with Wart, it's going to cost us a year, but I'll wait for you,' she said. 'It'll be worth it in the long run, you'll see.'

5

DANCING ON ICE

Walt lifted his whistle and blew a long blast that brought
Alex and Samantha to the side of the ice.

'What's up, Walt?' asked Alex. 'We're only half way
through.'

'Through is what you'll be if you skate a compulsory
like that,' said Walt.

'I didn't think it was that bad,' said Alex.

'It was very pretty,' said Walt. 'So tell me, what are the
judges looking for in the compulsories?' He gazed at Alex
because Samantha rarely spoke to him. The silence grew,
then, at last, Alex said: 'Style?'

Walt sighed and turned to Samantha.

'Style, expression, step placement, timing, flow, clean
movements and close proximity between partners,' reeled
off Samantha in a monotone.

'Exactly. So, little lady, that was supposed to be the
Argentine tango – yes?' Samantha didn't answer, just stood
there staring at him. Walt carried on, 'So, what was all
that business either side of the kilian?'

'I lost concentration,' she said.

'You were extemporizing! Adding bits in all over the place! You can't do that with the compulsories, leave it for the free.'

'For the free,' Samantha repeated flatly.

'Yes, the free,' said Walt, and, even though he was exasperated with her, his smile didn't reduce by a millimetre. 'And we can't work on the free until you get the compulsories right.' Samantha gave him a sweet smile, but didn't say a word.

'Shall we try again?' said Alex.

'No, call it a day – or rather an evening,' said Walt, glancing at his watch.

'There's another ten minutes yet,' said Alex.

'Leave it,' said Walt. 'Don't push so hard. We've plenty of time.' Samantha turned herself round and sat down on a rinkside bench to take her skates off without letting the blades touch the floor. Alex stayed on the ice.

'You don't think we could fit in another lesson?' suggested Alex.

'Hm, let's see. You've got the two mornings with me, Tuesdays and Thursdays, and now Friday evenings as well,' said Walt, though this was the first evening they had skated with him at the Coliseum. 'How many other evenings do you skate?'

'Mondays and Wednesdays, Liz's dance class,' said Alex, omitting to mention they always stayed long after the dance class had finished.

'So, that means you're skating five days a week?' said Walt. 'No, no, that's more than enough – too much, really.' Alex didn't say, but he was well aware that Samantha was skating considerably more than that. They hadn't discussed it in case it caused another row, but he thought she was skating up to seven nights a week.

'And you still don't want us training at the weekend?' asked Alex. Samantha glanced up at him but kept her loud silence. She turned to Walt to watch his answer.

'Well, it's a good idea to have a full two days' break from training each week to let your muscles relax,' said Walt. 'Anyway, the ice is too packed at the weekend to do any serious work.'

'I know, I didn't mean skating,' said Alex. 'I meant a training run, or a cycle ride — something along those lines.'

'Oh, no, you only develop your muscles in the wrong way. The sports aren't complementary,' said Walt. 'The skating you do will keep you perfectly fit, don't worry.' Walt was becoming disconcerted by Samantha's steady gaze. She gave him a smile and winked and he turned away.

'And now I've got some good news for you,' he said, producing two plastic bags from his holdall and handing them one each.

'What are they?' Alex asked.

'Official British Ice Dance Squad tracksuits,' said Walt. 'Sir Robert Sinclair got hold of me on the way in — you're officially in the squad, and there's another thing, though I'm not sure whether it's good news or not.'

'What?' demanded Alex.

'You've been invited to enter the British championships in three months' time,' said Walt.

'Wow, that's great, Walt — really great!' said Alex, excitedly. 'How about that, Samantha? Big time, eh?' She nodded briefly.

'How do you mean, it might not be good news?' she asked. Walt turned to her, surprised at her speaking to him for once.

'Because it's a bit early,' he said. 'You'd do better to go for it next year. It's just that there's a lack of good ice dancers this year.'

'Blow that,' said Alex. 'Of course we're going to enter.'

'Oh, well, I expect it'll be good experience.' Walt shrugged. 'I mean, you can't expect to get anywhere first time out but it'll get you noticed – I only hope it doesn't put you off!'

'Are Melodie Saxon and Lester Carmichael entering?' Samantha asked quietly.

'I've no idea,' he said. 'I should imagine so. Why? Are you worried about them?' Samantha shrugged.

'They're our closest rivals,' supplied Alex.

'Well, I think it'd be fairer to say you're their closest rivals,' said Walt. 'They are quite strong, yes, but they're a couple of years ahead. You can't hope to beat them yet awhile.'

'No,' said Alex shortly. He glanced worriedly at Samantha, wondering what she would say to this heresy, but she just beamed at him. This worried him even more.

'We'd better spend some time on our free dance, hadn't we, Walt?' said Alex.

'Yes, we'll have a play around with it next month,' said Walt. 'We'll soon string a few moves together – I told you, it all comes down to the compulsories.' He glanced at his watch again. 'Look, I'd better go. I've got to get right across London.'

28

'OK, Walt, thanks,' said Alex. 'See you on Tuesday.'
Samantha gave him a nod and he hurried off, still smiling.

Alex turned to Samantha. 'You might have thanked him,' he said.

'What for?' she said, sliding off the bench and facing him in her stockinged feet.

'For getting us entered in the British championships – and the British Ice Dance Squad!'

'You heard what he said, that was Sir Robert.'

'Maybe it was, but he wouldn't have even considered us if we hadn't got a professional trainer,' said Alex. 'What more do you want?'

'Nothing,' she said. 'It's you that's getting uptight, not me.'

'Oh, never mind. Look, Sue'll be waiting. I'll see you outside.'

Sue was Alex's special friend. She was a free skater, four years older than they were. She had once been Alex's baby-sitter and it had been Sue who had introduced him to skating in the first place. They were lucky it was on Friday that Walt had chosen to give them a lesson because Sue skated on Fridays at the Coliseum and could give them a lift. The Coliseum was right over the other side of London from their home rink. Sue was sitting, waiting in her battered Mini. They climbed in. Alex sat in the back so he could lie down.

'Sorry we're late, Sue,' he said. 'I've been looking for my shoes.'

'Not again,' sighed Sue. 'Which ones were they this time?'

29

'The left trainer I borrowed from Simon to replace the one I bought from that car boot sale that I lost last week,' said Alex bleakly.

'Simon?' grinned Sue. 'You mean Simon from the dance class? Does he know he lent it to you?'

Alex avoided answering. He lay on the back seat regarding his feet crossly. One was clad in an old slipper, which was all the porter could find for him.

'I don't understand it,' he said bitterly. 'It's every time I'm at the Coliseum – and only in the evenings.'

'Someone's having you on,' said Sue, starting the engine and driving out into the road.

'Ah – he's always losing something,' said Samantha unsympathetically. 'I can't keep up. Last year it was his shirt, now it's his shoe.'

'Someone's having a go at me,' said Alex. 'Who have I upset that's only there at night-time?'

'Where do they disappear from?' asked Sue.

'The anteroom, and it's not *them*. I wouldn't mind so much both of them going,' he said. 'It's just one each time.'

'So what we're looking for here is a one-legged skater with a grudge against you, who only skates at night?' said Samantha. 'Should be easy.'

'Can't you put them in your locker?' suggested Sue.

'No, the locker doesn't actually lock – anyway, we always change into our skates in the anteroom,' said Alex.

'It's lucky for us,' said Samantha. Sue didn't argue. All skaters seemed to have superstitions about little things bringing them luck.

'Anyway, that's why we're late,' said Alex. 'Sorry, Sue.'

'That's all right, you're not that late,' said Sue in a

friendly way. Not that she was likely to complain. Sue was much too easy-going for that.

They told her their news and even Samantha was excited now that Walt wasn't there. Sue was genuinely delighted for them even though she had never been invited into the British Skating Squad, or even been entered for a major competition, and now knew she never would be.

'How did your lesson go?' she asked. Sue was well aware of the difficult patch they were going through. To both Alex and Sue's surprise it was Samantha who answered.

'Fine, it was a good lesson,' she said.

'I can't believe it,' said Alex. 'You, actually praising Walt up!'

'Wart's good on the compulsory dances,' said Samantha. 'I never said he wasn't. He can do us a bit of good. We need his regimented approach.'

'What was all that about tonight, then?' Alex demanded. 'You adding bits in?'

'I was just checking whether he was watching,' said Samantha. 'He doesn't half the time, you know.'

'Ah, you're paranoid about him,' sighed Alex. Samantha gave a shrug and left a strained silence between them. Sue rushed to fill it:

'I'm skating in a competiton over at Bristol on Saturday,' she said.

'Bristol?' said Alex. 'I'll have to tell Toby.'

'Toby?' Samantha turned to look at him. 'Why Toby?'

'Because he was taking me to another one of his blasted football matches,' said Alex. He grinned. 'Thanks, Sue, I can get out of it now.'

Sue smiled. 'It's a long way, Alex, I'll understand if you can't make it.'

'Have I ever missed one?' said Alex. He tapped Samantha on the shoulder. 'Are you coming, motormouth?'

'Do you want me to?'

'That's a really intelligent thing to say, isn't it?' said Alex crossly. 'I was just thinking, you train that girl on Saturdays, don't you?'

'Oh, yes, sorry,' said Samantha. 'No, I'd love to come. Monica won't mind, she's not as enthusiastic, just lately, anyway.'

'Can you see if you can get us a couple of seats on the coach, Sue?' Alex asked.

'Actually, I've already booked them,' she admitted.

'See,' said Alex. He tapped Samantha on the shoulder again. 'See,' he repeated. She stuck her tongue out at him.

'There is another reason for you coming, though,' said Sue. 'The British Ice Dance champions are giving a demo in the afternoon to try to pick the crowd up.' Sue was trying to watch their reactions as well as drive the car. She was amply rewarded by the look on Samantha's face, a hungry look.

'Are they?' Samantha said, deliberately casual. 'Are they indeed?' She glanced at Alex and he gave her a significant nod.

6

FUTURE OPPOSITION?

The coach was quiet, the competitors all nervous. Alex and Samantha sat near the back. They were both feeling relaxed, almost glad that they weren't competing that day, but even so they were wearing their NISA track suits with 'British Ice Dance Squad' on the back. Nobody had questioned this. All the skaters would have done the same in their position, to proclaim their professional interest. What they would have been more surprised about were the two pairs of skates hidden away in Alex's sports bag.

Sue was sitting the other side of the gangway to Alex but she had withdrawn into herself and he left her firmly alone. Sue was an individual skater and the battle she had to fight was a lonely one. Alex was very glad that there was always Samantha to share his with him.

When they finally reached Bristol Ice Rink, the skaters disappeared towards the changing rooms. Alex and Samantha wandered around before sitting in the stands for a long and weary day. Sue needed support, even for the boring compulsory figures. The more interesting free

33

dances were later, after the crowd-drawing exhibition by the British Ice Dance champions.

One half of the British Ice Dance champions came into the 'Stars' anteroom whistling idly to himself, his skates dangling carelessly from one hand. Benjamin Trueman sat down on the most comfortable seat available, produced an apple from inside one skate, polished it meticulously on his sleeve, and proceeded to consume it with unhurried enjoyment.

The door half opened and through it came the sound of two voices whispering. Benjamin eyed it curiously, though never pausing in his attention to the apple. At last, two figures came into view and approached him nervously. Benjamin looked them up and down, took a last bite from his apple and slipped the core into the pocket of an offical's blazer hanging on the locker behind him. He yawned, stretched, and lazily started to put on his skates.

'I always wondered,' he said conversationally, 'wasn't it a bit hot skating in that cloak?'

The two looked taken aback. The boy spoke. 'You know who we are?'

'Alex Barnes and Samantha Stephens,' said Benjamin. He considered them for a long moment. 'But, you don't do figures and there's no dance competition today, so, why the skates? Oh, I get it, you had to wear them to get past Rambo on the door.'

'We didn't think we'd get in otherwise,' said Samantha.

'You were lucky. He only just let me past,' said Benjamin.

'We wanted to meet you,' said Samantha. 'If you mind us interrupting before you go on, just say.'

'It's only a demo,' said Benjamin. 'Sit down, will you? You're wearing the floor out.' They sat side by side on the bench opposite but neither could match Benjamin's relaxed posture.

'Don't you mind demos, then?' asked Alex. Benjamin finished lacing his last skate and slumped back against the locker and closed his eyes.

'That's a bit of a daft question, don't you think?' he said. 'If you don't know how I feel, you really shouldn't be doing this.'

'We know how you feel,' said Samantha.

'Yeah, well, it's just the way I handle it, OK?'

'How do you know us?' asked Alex.

'Be serious, it's my job,' said Benjamin. He shrugged. 'I've got a video of your Cloak and Dagger free dance.'

'Oh,' said Alex quietly. 'What did you think?'

'Brilliant,' said Benjamin. 'The idea anyway – hell of a lot better than your compulsories – they were crap!' He opened his eyes briefly and regarded them to see what their reaction would be to his words. 'You understand I'm being totally honest here?'

'We'd rather you were,' said Samantha. Alex didn't speak. He wasn't sure he agreed with her.

'Have you got many videos of other ice dancers?' she asked.

'Thousands, we study them for hours – you have to,' said Benjamin. 'Anyway, we like to keep an eye on any prospective opposition.'

'Ha!' said Alex.

'You wouldn't be here if you weren't serious contenders,' said Benjamin. They were saved from the embarrassment of a reply when the door opened and one of the most stunning girls they had ever seen walked into the room: the other half of the British Ice Dance champions had arrived.

'I thought you'd gone home,' said Benjamin. 'This is Alex Barnes, and Samantha Stephens. They've come to meet us – well, more me, I expect.' He waved airily towards the nervous pair opposite.

Belinda Thomas eyed them for a long moment, then the perfect lips in the perfect face opened:

'That's all I need!' she snapped, and stormed over to the far side of the room where she sat with her back to them to put on her skates.

Benjamin gave a delighted grin. 'Isn't she sweet?' he said. 'I mean doesn't she just – what's the word? – epitomize, the full flower of gentle femininity?' Benjamin seemed pleased with the word epitomize, and repeated it softly to himself. Alex and Samantha regarded him worriedly.

'I think we'd better go,' said Alex.

'Oh, don't worry about Belinda, she doesn't like ice skaters,' said Benjamin. This made him laugh and he did so amiably. He seemed disappointed when they didn't join in.

'If she's trying to psych herself up we'd better push off,' said Samantha.

'You've just done that for her,' said Benjamin. He gave

them his really nice grin. 'I told you, it's the way you handle it. Belinda's always like this before a competition, or a medal test, anything – even a demo. She has to fall out with someone, preferably the opposition, but it doesn't really matter – it can hardly be me, can it?'

'Oh, right,' said Alex, still unconvinced.

'About Cloak and Dagger,' said Samantha. 'You really thought it was all right?'

'Yes, I did,' said Benjamin. 'Oh, sure, you've got a lot of skating to learn, but whoever choreographed that free dance knew what they were doing.' Alex was about to say that it was Samantha but she deliberately forestalled him.

'We wanted to ask you about our training,' she said.

'Sure, you know the three rules of training?' said Benjamin. 'Practice, practice and practice!'

Alex forced a smile. 'We've got a new trainer, well, our first real trainer and he's got a few ideas that are different from what we're used to.'

'That's what a trainer's for, isn't it?' said Benjamin. 'Who is it? Anyone I know?'

'Walt Danvers.'

'Oh.' Benjamin didn't sound enthusiastic. 'He had a couple of World champions a few years back.'

'What we were wondering is, do you always do exactly what your trainer tells you?' asked Alex.

'It depends on the trainer. What matters is, do you get on with him? Are the three of you a team?' said Benjamin. 'Now, in our case, if Morris tells us to do something we absolutely don't want to do, we talk about it, thrash it out, argue – then do exactly what he said in the first place.

37

If he told us to go and lie down in front of a car transporter we'd probably do it. It'd be much less painful than disagreeing with him.'

Alex and Samantha both smiled, a little ruefully. 'What about if you had different ideas for your free dance?' Samantha asked.

'We do all the time. It's called creativity,' said Benjamin. 'It all works itself out in the end. I mean, Belinda has a few goes, storms off, that sort of thing – she hit me once, a real cracker!' He rubbed his cheek in remembrance.

'What about fitness training?' asked Alex. 'How much of that do you do?'

'Well, nowadays we skate so much we don't have time for more than a couple of miles running at lunch times – perhaps a bit of cycling at weekends,' said Benjamin. 'We're both at Birmingham University and they're very good about fitting in training times.'

The door crashed open and a small man came stomping into the room.

'Now, I *should* push off if I were you,' said Benjamin. 'Morris won't like you being here at all.'

'Oh, right,' said Alex, getting to his feet. 'Look, er, thanks.'

'Any time,' said Benjamin expansively. 'I'll see you at the British championships.'

'How do you know we're entered?' asked Samantha. 'It's supposed to be a secret. We've only just been told ourselves.'

'Be serious,' said Benjamin, leaning back and shutting his eyes again. 'It's my job.'

38

Morris was eyeing them suspiciously so they hurriedly made their way back to the safety of the main rink.

'What were they doing here?' Morris demanded.

'That was Alex Barnes and Samantha—'

'I know who it was!' snapped Morris. 'What did they want?'

'My autograph,' grinned Benjamin. 'You can have it as well if you want.'

Morris growled at him. Benjamin opened his eyes, leaned forward and said seriously, 'No harm in having a chat, Morris.'

'No?' said Morris, then appeared to change the subject. 'The Olympics are next year.'

'I did hear something about that,' said Benjamin, sarcastically.

'And who are your main opposition?'

'Charlie Varker and Tammy Man, of course.'

'And they're retiring, win or lose – right?'

'Well, going professional.'

'Same thing,' said Morris. 'So, what about four years after that? The next Olympics? Who's going to be the opposition then?'

'Hell, Morris, I don't know,' said Benjamin. 'That's five years away! We'll have to see who comes up from the ranks.'

'We will, indeed.' Morris nodded towards the door through which Alex and Samantha had just disappeared. 'If those two can get their act together, keep their problems off the ice – it could well be them.'

Benjamin considered, then gave a nod. 'Maybe,' he said.

39

'I'm telling you,' said Morris. 'So you watch what you say!' He made for the door. 'Three minutes,' he threw back over his shoulder.

Benjamin gazed after him, and gave his wonderful smile. He got reluctantly to his feet and strolled over to where Belinda was standing, pretending to study a poster on the wall. He put his arms around her from behind and gave her cheek a kiss.

'Come on, then, sweetheart,' he said gently. 'Let's go and show them what it's all about.'

7

GOOD LOSERS?

Alex saw Mr Dodd coming up the main corridor towards him. He swore. He owed the physics teacher a project and had been avoiding him all week. Alex glanced around then ducked through the door of the office. He breathed a sigh of relief when Mr Dodd went past without looking in.

'Ah, Alex, how nice to see you,' said a voice, and he whirled to find his chemistry lecturer, Mrs Kennedy, giving him her sweetest smile. Alex didn't trust the smile one inch – she had a bite like an adder.

'Oh. I'm sorry, Mrs Kennedy, I've got to rush. I've got a lecture to go to,' he tried.

'No, you haven't! Brief reference to your timetable will inform you that you're supposed to be in mine,' said Mrs Kennedy.

'Well, you're not in it, are you?' said Alex, with some justification.

'I wasn't aware that it stipulated in my contract of employment that I had to justify my whereabouts to you,' said Mrs Kennedy mildly. 'But, if that is indeed the case, then it is incumbent on me to inform you that I'm just doing some photocopying while the class finishes off an experiment before lunch – is that all right?'

'Yes, Mrs Kennedy,' said Alex. Then he added, 'Thank you,' though he wasn't sure why.

'Now we come to the interesting bit,' said Mrs Kennedy. 'We've established why I'm not there, so, how about you?'

'I'm sorry, I came in late,' said Alex. 'I overslept.'

Mrs Kennedy glanced at her watch. 'Eleven forty-five. My word, Alex, that's some lie-in.'

'Look, I'm trying here,' said Alex. 'How about, I had a dental appointment?'

Mrs Kennedy shook her head sadly. 'Over used,' she said. 'That's the third time this term already.'

'OK – how about, my mother was kidnapped by Iraqi terrorists and held to ransom? And I had to try and raise the money?'

'Marginally better,' said Mrs Kennedy. 'How about, you haven't done your homework again and are avoiding me until you've had time to copy it off somebody?'

Alex gazed at her with wide-eyed innocence. 'Mrs Kennedy, how you can think such a thing! You must know me better than that. I'm shocked, yes shocked – to accuse me of such, such . . . well, I'm lost for words.'

'Yes, but am I right?' she said.

'Absolutely – spot on!' said Alex. He added in an aggrieved tone, 'You took all the books in so I couldn't copy it off anybody.'

Mrs Kennedy had the grace to smile. She picked up the stack of sheets the photocopier had been churning out and pushed past him to the door.

'Friday, Alex,' she said.

'Aw, but Mrs—'

'Friday, or I won't mark it.' Then she was gone. Alex sighed then glanced at the college secretary who had been watching the scene with great enjoyment.

'Why do you think she uses all those long words?' he said.

'Perhaps she's thinking of going into politics,' offered the secretary. 'Are you here for any specific reason, Alex? Or are you just hiding?'

'I'm just hiding,' he said. 'No, there was something, have you had any training shoes handed in?'

'Where did you lose them?'

'The Coliseum,' Alex admitted.

'It's hardly likely, is it?' she said.

'No, I just thought you might have a spare pair hanging about,' said Alex. 'Someone keeps pinching mine – well, one of them, anyway. I must've upset someone and they've got a weird sense of humour.'

'There's a pair in the lost property locker that have been there for years,' said the secretary. 'They should fit you, but they're awfully tatty.'

'That's all right, they'll only get pinched on Friday night,' said Alex. 'Thanks, you've saved my life.' He went off shaking his head. 'I think it's the porter,' were the last words she heard him say.

Alex made his way along the danger zone of the main corridor to the relative safety of the maths department. Cautiously, he glanced through the glass panel of one of the lecture rooms and sighed with exasperation. It simply wasn't his day. His maths lecturer was taking Samantha's class. Samantha was nowhere in sight so he made faces at

Zoe, one of her friends. At last she noticed him and he mouthed: 'Where's Samantha?' at her. She shrugged, so he mouthed: 'Is she in school?' but this time Zoe couldn't get it and then the door opened and a testy maths lecturer was confronting him.

'What is it now, Alex?' he demanded. 'This is taking eccentricity too far! If you can't be bothered to turn up for your own lectures, at least have the courtesy not to come to other people's!'

'Sorry, Mr Thatcher. I really need to have a word with Zoe,' said Alex. 'It's very important.' Mr Thatcher sighed but gestured to Zoe and shut the door very firmly indeed on them.

'What were all the charades for?' Zoe demanded. 'You've really put me in good with Maggie there.'

'Sorry. I just want to know if Samantha is in college?'

'Yeah, she was at registration but I haven't seen her since,' said Zoe. 'She was in a bit of a funny mood.'

'Oh, that'll make a nice change,' said Alex. 'So, where is she?' A light came on in Alex's brain. 'Oh, of course – cheers, Zoe.' He gave her a quick kiss and ran off up the corridor. Zoe stared after him.

'Gee, thanks Alex,' she said.

The drama department was right over the other side of the college, next to the theatre, and off to one side was the tiny dance studio. Alex could hear the music from the end of the corridor and knew he had guessed right. He eased the door open and slid inside. As a performer himself Alex knew better than to interrupt when she was dancing.

Samantha, dressed in a leotard that was soaking with sweat, was creating a dramatic, moody dance. He sat on the floor watching with pleasure as she ad libbed moves, fitting them to the music, using her whole personality to create an entire atmosphere. At last the music died, leaving her collapsed in a heap in the middle of the floor.

'And what's your dad going to say if you mess up your GCSEs again?' Alex said. She jumped at his words. She had been so wrapped up in her dancing that she hadn't even noticed the door open.

'Oh, Alex.' She came to her feet and he tossed her a towel. She dried herself off avoiding his eyes.

'You know what your dad said: he'll stop you skating if you don't do better at college than you did at school!'

'Don't be ridiculous,' she said testily.

'OK, so I'm being ridiculous. I know that he has as much chance of controlling you as I have, but seriously, Samantha, don't you think you should get them for your own sake?'

'Stop fussing,' she sighed. 'I'll do better this time. I just needed a morning off.'

'I noticed. What's wrong?'

'Nothing's wrong!'

'Sure, there isn't! You've been a sheer delight to know this past week,' he said. 'Ever since we saw Benjamin and Belinda skate you've been like it.'

'I haven't, you're imagining it.'

'Well, so's everybody else then! You wouldn't even speak to me on the coach home,' he said. 'And what you said to that poor man in the motorway café was rich even for you.'

'Well, the fool asked me if we were football supporters!'

Alex put his hands on her damp shoulders. 'Come

on, stop pratting about,' he said. 'I'm your partner – remember? Is it something to do with Benjamin and Belinda?'

She looked down and gave a tiny nod.

'Well, what? I thought they were great.'

'Great? They were brilliant!' she said. 'We'll never be able to skate like that.'

'Oh, we will,' sighed Alex, realizing what was bothering her at last. 'They must be four years older than us.'

'That's the point, not that they're four years ahead of us, but they're *only* four years ahead of us!' she said. 'Don't you see? They'll always be there.' She shook her head. 'We can't beat them, Alex.'

'Frankly, to be beaten by skaters of that calibre is no embarrassment,' he said. She shook him off angrily.

'I told you before, I skate to win or there's no point – anything but first place is losing!' There was a long pause, then he put his hands back on her shoulders.

'Listen, Samantha,' he said, his voice gentle. 'Where does it say we won't get that good?'

'Oh, we'll get the steps,' she said, 'but you saw them out there, they weren't skating, they were making love! We can't skate that way.'

'We might.'

'No! Whatever we feel for one another, that's not how we are – anyway—' she broke off; then, 'I choreograph our stuff – yes? In spite of Wart.'

'Of course you do.'

'Well, I can't choreograph that sort of thing.'

'OK, then, don't,' said Alex. 'Look, they are into all this

romantic stuff. So what? Our strong point – your strong point – is telling a story. Doing something really original, agreed?'

'Well, yes—'

'Something like Apache, or Cloak and Dagger, even Benjamin said Cloak and Dagger was brilliant. When we skated Cloak and Dagger we won everything we even looked at,' said Alex. 'Since Torvill and Dean did Bolero, everyone's going in that direction, but we've never run with the crowd. Why should we now?'

'Yeah, the Duchesnays did that Jungle dance thing,' she said slowly. She shrugged. 'They lost with it though, didn't they?'

'So we do one better,' said Alex. 'Come on, Samantha, you can do it.'

She eyed him for a moment, then, 'Wart won't like it,' she said.

'Oh, that'll upset you,' he said sarcastically. 'Don't mind about Walt, he's more interested in the compulsories.'

'OK,' she said in a small voice. 'Sorry, Alex.'

'Don't worry about it,' said Alex. 'Show me a good loser and I'll show you a loser – do you know who said that?'

'John McEnroe?' Samantha offered.

'He should have – actually, it was Paul Newman,' said Alex. 'I bet Belinda Thomas isn't a good loser!'

'No,' said Samantha. 'I tell you one area where we can't match those two.'

'Where?'

'They've got the world's best trainer.'

8

BEING NICE
TO WALT

Samantha's left skate hit a rut in the ice and went away
from her, but she simply relaxed into the fall and went
into front splits.

'Now, this is no time to have a sit down,' said Alex.

'This damned ice!' Samantha said crossly, scrambling to
her feet. 'It's like skating on a frozen rugby pitch at night.
I got used to skating mornings.'

'It's good practice. We might be drawn last in the British
championships,' said Alex.

'Even if we're not drawn last, that's where we'll be at
the end,' said Samantha. 'With this free dance, anyway.'

'Oh, give it a chance, we've only had two sessions on it
so far.'

'Come on, Alex, it's useless. Even you can see that!'

'What does that mean? Even me?'

She shrugged. 'It means even though you're in awe of
Wart, you should be able to see that this free dance could
be skated by a pair of beginners.'

'Considering the standard Wart – I mean Walt – is used
to training, I expect that's exactly what we seem to him,

48

beginners,' said Alex. He took her somewhat roughly in his arms and they started their free dance again from where Samantha had fallen. After a minute he said, 'I'm not in awe of him.'

'Either that or he drugs you! You won't hear a word said against him.'

'That's not true either,' said Alex. He sighed. 'It's just that I haven't got a rich daddy.'

'Translate that for me, will you?'

'Even if I could convince my parents that I needed a professional trainer, which I can't, there is no way they could afford to pay for one,' said Alex. 'I know Walt's not perfect but he's the one hope I've got of ever getting a top line trainer.'

'My dad would pay for one.'

'I know he would, that's the whole point,' said Alex testily.

'So we are stuck with Wart because of your pride?'

'Sense of responsibility more than pride, I would have said.'

'Garbage! It's pride,' she said. 'Oh, Alex, I understand how you feel but we can't afford this. My dad likes spending money on me, let him – it makes him feel loved. We'll reward him with a gold medal one day.'

'We can do it for free with Walt.'

'No, we can't.' She shook her head. 'Listen, I've heard that Benjamin Trueman has worse trouble than you. Belinda's parents used to pay for everything until they got a sponsor.'

'Well, yours aren't going to!' Alex snapped. 'Pity I'm not Lester Carmichael, isn't it?'

'Why?'

'His dad's a millionaire, didn't you know?' said Alex. 'They've got everything – and I do mean everything! When they go to a competition they fly there in his private helicopter.'

'You can't buy a gold medal,' said Samantha.

'No, but it helps,' said Alex.

Their free dance fizzled to an ending that left them facing each other.

'That's it, is it?' she said sarcastically. 'Wow, that'll have the crowd on it's feet!'

'Well, why don't you talk to Walt . . . nicely . . . about it?'

'You don't talk to warts, you use wart remover,' she said. Then, at the look on his face, 'Oh, all right, I'll be nice to him.' They skated across to where Walt was standing talking to somebody. When they got closer they saw it was Sir Robert Sinclair, president of NISA.

'Best behaviour now.' Alex gave Samantha a nudge with his elbow. 'Mind your language.'

'Bum,' she said charmingly. But even Samantha realized that Sir Robert was an important force in ice skating and she put on her best smile, which, to be absolutely accurate, wasn't much. Samantha was a very attractive girl, but in a tense, dramatic sort of way. Smiling wasn't her best expression.

'Hello, Sir Robert,' said Alex.

'Hello, Alex . . . Samantha,' said Sir Robert. 'How are you three getting on?' Samantha's smile slipped and she glanced around as though looking for the third person Sir Robert was talking about. Alex hurriedly stepped in.

'Fine, thank you,' he said.

'Good, well, I'll leave you alone then,' he said. 'I've just been giving Mr Danvers here all the information on the British championships.' He nodded and smiled, then strode across the ice to speak to somebody else. Sir Robert was one of those people who was always in a hurry. Samantha turned to Walt.

'This free dance is useless,' she said. 'There's more chance of Belinda Thomas winning Sports Personality of the Year than of us winning the British championships with it.'

Alex turned an incredulous look on her. 'That was nice?' he demanded.

'As nice as it gets,' she said. She turned back to Walt. 'Well?'

'Of course it won't win the British championships,' said Walt. 'I've told you, it's a very bad idea you entering the British championships in the first place – it's much too early.'

'Sir Robert doesn't seem to think so,' said Alex quietly.

'Yes, and, like I told you, there's a lack of good ice dancers this year,' said Walt. 'You could easily withdraw, then have a whole year to practise before the next one.'

Alex glanced at Samantha's furious face; he kept his voice level.

'Walt, everyone thinks we should enter: Liz, Sir Robert, even Benjamin Trueman.'

'That's rather the point, isn't it? You'll be up against Benjamin Trueman and Belinda Thomas,' said Walt. 'It's going to cost a lot as well – there's the official practices.

And it means going away for the weekend: train fares, hotel bills!'

'We'll manage it,' said Samantha. 'Won't we, Alex?'

He sighed. 'Yes, we'll manage it,' he said.

'Oh, well, it's your decision,' said Walt. 'Now, what's wrong with your free dance?'

'It's a bit simple,' said Alex.

'It's pathetic!' said Samantha. 'It makes us look like wallies – that might not bother Superstar here, but I don't like looking like a wally!'

'I'd rather have you skating something simple and doing it really well than coming to grief on something more complicated,' said Walt. He sighed at the look on Samantha's face. 'OK, we'll try and beef it up a bit – right? Tuesday morning, let me have a few ideas.'

'Are we finishing for the night?' asked Alex.

'Yes, I think it'll do us all good,' said Walt. 'Oh, and yes, Sir Robert really came to tell you that the whole dance squad is meeting at Nottingham Ice Rink next Saturday.'

'You mean for an official practice?' asked Alex.

'No, it's more so that NISA can have another look at you all, make sure they've chosen right.'

'But our free is nowhere near good enough to show yet,' protested Samantha.

'No, you just do a couple of compulsory dances,' said Walt. 'Then in the afternoon you get to skate with Charlie Varker and Tammy Mann.'

'We what?' Samantha gasped.

'You each get five minutes with them,' said Walt.

'They're doing a tour and NISA have persuaded them to give you an idea of how the World champions skate.'

'How are we getting there?' asked Alex.

'Train, presumably,' said Walt.

'Ah,' said Alex, looking thoughtful.

9

SOMETHING TO DO WITH ICE SKATING

Alex usually walked Samantha home after a night-time session. This was the time when they really talked, when no one else was there. Tonight, though, Alex was unusually quiet. Samantha glanced at him a couple of times before she spoke.

'Bit of good news about Saturday?'

He jumped. 'Yeah,' he said.

'Skating with Charlie Varker and Tammy Mann?'

'Oh, yeah – great,' he said.

'And NISA's going to have another look at us,' she said.

'Yeah,' said Alex. He kicked a stone that was lying inoffensively in the road.

'It's a chance for us to show off our compulsories,' she said. 'They're tons better than the last time.'

'Yeah,' said Alex again.

'It'll be nice to meet the rest of the squad as well, won't it?' she said. He didn't answer so she hit him with her elbow. 'You're supposed to say "yeah" now,' she offered.

'Eh?' he said, surprised.

'Wrong! Not, eh – yeah.'

He turned to look at her. 'What are you on about?' he demanded.

'Nothing,' she said. 'Thank you for walking me home.'

'What?'

'That's my home – ' she pointed – 'you know, where I live?'

'I know,' he said. She looked at him and gave a small smile. Sometimes they kissed goodnight, but not always, and she knew they wouldn't tonight.

'You go that way,' she pointed again.

'I know,' he said testily. She watched him for a minute then called to his back:

'See you tomorrow?'

'Yeah,' came floating back to her from the darkness.

Samantha sighed with exasperation and went into the house. She stopped by the hall mirror and arranged her fringe to give her her very best 'little girl' look. It was wasted; when she went into the lounge only her mother was there, sitting in front of the fire doing the *Telegraph* crossword.

'Hello, darling,' said Mrs Stephens.

'Dad not home yet?' Samantha said, slumping down onto the settee.

'No, he had to go to Birmingham,' said Mrs Stephens. She frowned at the newspaper. 'I don't suppose you know which Britain's first colony was?' She looked up at her daughter and shook her head. 'No, silly of me. Of course you don't. It's not about ice skating.'

'You could ask Dad when he gets in,' suggested Samantha.

'Why? It's not about accountancy, or golf either,' said Mrs Stephens. 'Tired, darling?'

'Chance'd be a fine thing,' said Samantha. 'We don't work hard enough to get tired, nowadays.'

'I'm glad to hear it,' said Mrs Stephens, absently.

'Mummy,' said Samantha. 'We've been asked to Nottingham Ice Rink this Saturday to meet Charlie Varker and Tammy Mann.'

'By we, I presume you mean Alex and you?'

'Yes, of course,' said Samantha. 'We get the chance to skate with them.'

'Bermuda,' said Mrs Stephens, mysteriously.

'Bermuda?' demanded Samantha. 'What do you mean, Bermuda?'

'It was our first colony,' said Mrs Stephens, writing the answer in.

'Oh, good,' muttered Samantha. She tried again. 'It's great news about Saturday, isn't it?'

'I don't know,' said Mrs Stephens. She laid down the paper. 'How are you getting there?'

'Train, of course.'

'Are you sure?' said her mother seriously. 'You're not going to try and get your father to drive you there, are you?'

'No, Mummy, of course not,' said Samantha. 'I never ask him to drive me anywhere.'

'Oh, Samantha, this is me you're talking to.' Her mother sighed. 'You know your father, he'd do anything for you. You'll just stand there all innocent and mention something about how long the train journey is, and you know what'll happen.'

'That's not fair,' said Samantha. 'I never do anything like that.'

'Why have you put your hair in that silly way then?' demanded her mother. Samantha avoided answering. She traced the pattern of the carpet with the toe of one of her trainers.

'He's working very hard at the moment and I don't want him driving up to Nottingham and back on his weekend off,' said Mrs Stephens. 'He's supposed to be playing golf this Saturday, and I want you to promise you won't try anything.'

'OK,' muttered Samantha. There was silence for a minute before she added in a small voice, 'He always says he doesn't mind driving.'

'Samantha!'

'Yes, yes – I said OK,' said Samantha.

'Who's going anyway? Just you and Alex?'

'No, all the trainers will be there too. Wart ...' She broke off for a minute. When she started speaking again it was in a much warmer voice, '. . . Walter's coming with us.'

'Walter?'

'Yes, you know, our new trainer?'

'I thought you didn't like him?' said her mother.

'Of course I do,' said Samantha. 'Everybody likes Walter – especially the girls.'

'Do they?' said Mrs Stephens coldly.

'Yeah, they're all sick as parrots because I've . . . I mean, we've got him as a trainer,' said Samantha reverently. Mrs

Stephens was so taken aback she forgot to tell Samantha not to say, yeah.

'How old is this Walter?' she asked slowly.

'About forty, I think — but he doesn't look it,' said Samantha.

'Is he married?' said Mrs Stephens.

'Walter! Married?' said Samantha. She laughed. 'Not any more, anyway.' She got to her feet and stretched. 'Well, I'm off to bed. Say goodnight to Dad for me, will you?'

'Yes,' said Mrs Stephens.

'It's not a question of me asking them,' said Samantha. 'They insisted.'

'I don't believe you,' said Alex.

'Do you think I'd lie to you, Alex?' she demanded.

'Don't be ridiculous,' said Alex. 'You always lie to me — you lie to everybody!'

'I don't!' she said, so loudly that everybody in the coffee bar looked. She took a sip of her black coffee and waited until everyone had gone back to normal. It was morning break at the sixth-form college, though that didn't strictly apply to Samantha because she had only just got in.

'I only lie when it's necessary,' she said more gently. 'Something to do with ice skating.'

'I know that — and this is to do with ice skating.' There was a pause, before he asked seriously: 'Did he really offer?'

'Yes! Yes! Yes!' she said. 'It was Mum's idea, actually, not mine — honestly! They want to meet Walter — Wart.'

'Walter?' demanded Alex incredulously. 'Who the hell's Walter?'

'Just a slip of the tongue,' said Samantha. 'Look, Alex, they obviously want to meet our new trainer. They can't do that at six o'clock in the morning so this is the perfect opportunity. Mum suggested they drive us up to Nottingham and they can have a day out, go for a meal, that sort of thing.'

'Well, if that's true . . .' said Alex. 'It's just that we can't keep getting them to drive us all over the place. It's not fair – you know my mum and dad won't.'

'Your dad's car isn't reliable enough to drive as far as Nottingham,' said Samantha.

'You know that's not the reason,' said Alex. 'He doesn't approve of me skating as it is.'

Samantha for once had the tact to change the subject.

'Right, that's agreed then?' she said. 'My dad takes us all to Nottingham on Saturday?'

'All right,' he said. 'To tell you the truth, it gets me out of a bit of a hole – I'm absolutely broke and I couldn't afford the train fare.'

'Couldn't you?' she said.

'No, I've been worried about it,' he said. 'Sorry if I was a bit off last night, but that was the reason.'

'I didn't notice anything,' said Samantha absently. 'Say, I bet you don't know what Britain's first colony was?'

'Bermuda, wasn't it?' said Alex, surprised at the question.

Samantha frowned, then shook her head. 'No,' she said.

10

ADVICE FROM BELINDA

Alex and Samantha sat in the front row of Nottingham Ice Rink, the rink that had produced Jayne Torvill and Christopher Dean. But today there were two new figures out on the ice, the Americans, Charlie Varker and Tammy Mann. They were demonstrating the Argentine tango to the handful of skaters scattered around the rink. The rink was closed to the public until noon when the doors would be opened and Charlie and Tammy would skate the free dance that had won them the World championships the previous year.

'Where's the skin infection?' Samantha asked.

'Eh?' Alex said, turning to her in surprise.

'Wart.'

'Oh – he must still be with your mum and dad,' said Alex. 'They seem to be getting on OK, don't they?'

'Yes,' said Samantha, unenthusiastically.

'Hey, why was your mum so mad with you in the car?' asked Alex. 'She was all right until we picked up Walt. After that I thought she was going to hit you.'

'It's her hormones,' said Samantha. She was searching the rink with her eyes. 'Have you seen Melodie Saxon and Lester Carmichael?'

'No, but I tell you who is here.' He nudged Samantha and pointed out a short stocky figure with a grumpy expression.

'Morris Rose,' said Samantha. 'Belinda Thomas and Benjamin Trueman's trainer – oh, look ...' she breathed as the pair on the ice flew past. 'Did you see that?'

'Yes, they're not bad are they?' said Alex. 'See how they're absolutely together on the turn?' They watched in admiration as the two skaters flowed into another compulsory dance without even a break in rhythm.

'Is that his name? Rose?' asked Alex.

''Course it is, didn't you know? He's one of *the* names in the skating world,' she said. 'Do you think that means Benjamin and Belinda are here?'

'I doubt it,' said Alex. 'They're Charlie Varker and Tammy Mann's biggest rivals, aren't they?'

'Well, them, and the Russian pair,' said Samantha. 'No, you're right, they couldn't really be here, could they? They've got to pretend that they don't care how Charlie Varker and Tammy Mann skate.'

'They probably don't,' said Alex. 'They must have seen them skate a hundred times before.'

Right up high, in the controller's office that looked out over the ice, Belinda Thomas was standing regarding Benjamin Trueman. She had an exasperated look on her face as he tracked the couple down on the ice with a video camera.

'Do you want me to do it?' she demanded.

'I can manage,' he said shortly.

'Um – if you get it wrong Morris will have your tripes out!'

'Go and teach your grandmother to suck eggs!' said Benjamin, deliberately using one of Belinda's expressions.

'Don't lean too far forward or they'll see you,' said Belinda.

'Don't be so daft,' said Benjamin. He heaved a sigh of relief and laid the camera down as Charlie Varker and Tammy Mann came to the end of their dance. 'Do you really think they don't know we're here?'

'Well, they might think we're here, but they don't know do they?'

'Of course they do!' said Benjamin. 'Look at Morris prowling around down there like a tiger who has lost her cubs. He's not fooling anybody! I don't know why we don't all video our own free dances and supply everybody with copies. Save everybody all this trouble.'

'Tigress,' said Belinda.

'Eh?'

'Tigresses have cubs, not tigers,' said Belinda. She glanced down at the ice. 'Watch out, I think the children are about to perform.' Benjamin picked up the camera in readiness as the watching pairs of skaters were invited onto the ice to warm up.

'And we just want Melodie Saxon and Lester Carmichael, and Samantha Stephens and Alex Barnes?' asked Benjamin.

'Well, they're really the only potential competition here,' she said. 'You'll have to be careful though – when they pair up with Charlie and Tammy, they'll be skating on different sides of the rink.'

'I'll manage,' grunted Benjamin. 'Tell me, who do you reckon are going to be the main problems in the future?'

'I'm not sure,' said Belinda. 'I hope it's Alex and Samantha.'

'Why? Do you think they'll be easier to beat?'

'I wasn't thinking along those lines,' said Belinda. She came and stood close to him so she could see the skaters below. 'It's just that I can't stand Melodie Saxon or Lester Carmichael!'

Back down on the ice, the rink manager beckoned to Alex and Samantha. They hurried over.

'Alex and Sam, isn't it?' he asked.

'Samantha,' she said, gently.

'Yes. We're going by alphabetical order so you're on first,' he said. 'Now you really must have no more than five minutes, there's the whole squad to get through before twelve o'clock.'

'Just a minute,' rapped a voice. They all turned to find a very smart lady in a very smart suit marching towards them.

'Mr Evans.' Her voice was a bite.

'Oh, no, that's all I needed.' The rink manager sighed.

'Melodie and Lester are quite ready to go on now,' she said.

'Right then, Ms Barrett, I'll put them on after Alex and Samantha here.'

'Oh, nonsense, they're not going to hang around all day,' she snapped. 'We've got appointments this afternoon – I've already informed them that they would be on first.'

'Perhaps you should've informed me as well,' said the rink manager sarcastically. 'They're jumping the queue by going second. I've just been telling Alex and Samantha that we're taking everybody in alphabetical order.'

'Mr Evans, may I remind you that Melodie and Lester are the leading contenders here today and as such should have the right to skate on the best surface possible' – she gave Alex and Samantha a derisory glance – 'before this pair here churn up the ice.'

Samantha said one short but extremely descriptive noun. The woman blinked.

'Charming,' she said.

'Just my opinion,' said Samantha and gave an innocent smile. Alex put his arm around her shoulders and steered her away.

'It's all right, Mr Evans,' he said over his shoulder. 'Let the, er . . . leading contenders, go first. We don't mind.' Before the rink manager could reply, Ms Barrett gave a sniff.

'I'll go and get them,' she said, and marched away, the high heels she was wearing leaving marks on the rubber flooring.

'No need to thank us,' Alex shouted after her, but she ignored him.

'Who the hell was that?' Samantha demanded. 'Their trainer?'

'No, she's their – well, their manageress,' said Mr Evans, with a half smile.

'You're kidding?' said Alex. 'What do they want a manageress for?'

64

'It's another way of wasting money, I suppose,' said the rink manager.

Walt appeared from nowhere and came over. The rink manager immediately abandoned them.

'What was all that about?' asked Walt.

'Melodie Saxon and Lester Carmichael seem to think they have a divine right to go on first,' snapped Samantha.

'Don't let it worry you,' said Walt soothingly. He tried to put his arm around Samantha but she shrugged him off.

'It damn well does worry me,' she snapped. 'If we keep letting them walk all over us that's exactly what they'll do in competition.' She regarded Walt levelly for a moment before adding: 'But what worries me even more is that neither of you two seem to think it matters.'

Melodie Saxon and Lester Carmichael may well have been ready but they still kept everybody waiting, including the World champions, before they put in an appearance. Then, true to form, they stayed on the ice much longer than Mr Evans had stipulated. In fact, it took another argument between the rink manager and Ms Barrett before they finally came off. Samantha had wanted to get involved in the argument but Alex had held her back.

And, now, when their concentration had been totally destroyed, Alex and Samantha were asked out onto the ice. Alex was in a bad mood. He was much slower to anger than Samantha, but the arrogance of Melodie Saxon and Lester Carmichael, and their manageress, had finally got to him. He was frowning as he skated towards his temporary partner, half wondering whether Samantha was right.

65

'Wow,' said Tammy Mann, giving him the most lovely smile. 'You look really pleased to see me.'

'Oh, er, I'm sorry,' said Alex. 'It's not you, it's just something that happened a minute ago.'

'I know, I just met them,' she grinned. 'Come on, let's see if we can stay on our feet for a couple of minutes.'

She was bigger than the waif-like Samantha and not as 'dancified'. But her skating was absolutely right, her edges perfect and her confidence amazing. The surprising thing was that Alex didn't feel he was skating with the World champion, superstar of the skating world. She was so easy going and natural, it was just like a normal practice session. He met her eyes and she gave him another warm smile and this time he immediately responded.

'That's better,' she said. 'You're supposed to enjoy skating, you know.'

'Sorry,' he said. 'Look, I'm forgetting my manners. I didn't even introduce myself, I'm . . .'

'Alex Barnes,' she supplied. 'And that's Samantha Stephens over there.'

'How did you know?'

'I've got a video of you, of course,' she grinned again. With her, it was almost a permanent expression. 'That Cloak and Dagger free you did at the Seniors.'

'Oh, no,' muttered Alex. 'Look, we haven't been together that long.'

'Don't apologize, it was an excellent free dance,' she said.

'Do you mean that?'

'Of course,' she said. 'The idea was great, the choreography superb, and as for the timing – you hit the Seniors right when the music was in the charts!'

'What about the skating?'

'It was OK – it was more than OK for your age and level.' She gave him a little shake. 'Hey, relax will you? Five years ago we were in exactly the same position as you are now, only it was us who were unranked, dancing with Torvill and Dean.' Alex blinked, he hadn't thought of this.

'Who's your trainer?' she asked.

'Mr Danvers.'

'Walt Danvers?' She was surprised. They went around the ice again switching to the waltz as the music changed.

'What's wrong with him?' Alex said, after a minute.

'Walt? Nothing! He knows what he's doing, does Walt Danvers,' she said. 'It's just that you must be very rich.'

'You have no idea how funny that is,' said Alex.

'Your partner then?'

'Not really,' said Alex. 'No, Walt trains us for free.'

'No!' she said positively.

'He does, honest. He offered.'

Tammy stopped them in the middle of the ice as the music died away. They stood there waiting for a minute while it was changed.

'Alex,' she said levelly, 'Walt Danvers doesn't work for free, believe me. He's only in Britain because he's out of favour back home at the moment.'

'Why? What did he do?'

'Oh, nothing that's actually wrong, you understand. It's just that he dumped the couple he was training a month before the World championships and took on a new pair because he was offered more money. The couple were left stranded and lost out. No, Alex, what Walt Danvers does is never for free!'

'NISA must be paying Walt, obviously,' said Alex.

'Obviously,' said Samantha.

They were leaning on Samantha's parents' car watching as Mr and Mrs Stephens said an enthusiastic goodbye to Walt. He wasn't travelling back with them because he said he had some business in the Midlands. Samantha had a sour look on her face.

'Well, if what Tammy was saying is right, someone's paying,' said Alex.

'Tammy, is it?' said Samantha. 'Well, it's easy enough to find out. We'll just ask Sir Robert next time we see him.'

'We can't march up to Sir Robert Sinclair and demand to know whether he's paying our trainer!'

'I can,' said Samantha. She sighed in exasperation thinking that her parents were never going to finish talking to Walt. 'Come on,' she muttered. 'You don't have to fall in love with each other!'

'How did you get on with Charlie Varker?' asked Alex.

'Oh, he's gorgeous,' she said, with an evil grin.

'That's not what I meant.'

Samantha shrugged. 'To tell you the truth I didn't want to like him, but it's impossible not to. He's a really nice bloke.'

'I know, she was lovely too,' said Alex. 'If they're that nice all the time, how on earth did they become World champions?'

'I don't suppose they're quite as nice as that when

68

they're competing,' said Samantha. 'Did you learn anything?'

'Oh yes – I'll show you later,' he said. 'Though it's more the attitude – how good you've got to be more than any specific steps.'

'Yeah, and the speed,' said Samantha. 'He seemed to accelerate from nought to fifty in one step.'

'They know of us,' said Alex.

'Yes, Charlie said,' said Samantha. 'They've got a video of Cloak and Dagger. Must be from the Seniors. I know we were being videoed there.'

'Tammy says we should be watching videos of other skaters all the time,' said Alex. 'I don't know where we're supposed to get hold of them.'

'Charlie said that Wart should have given them to us as a matter of course,' said Samantha. 'I do watch the famous dances on video, but I didn't realize there were others available. What did you think of their free dance?'

'Brilliant – well, no, not brilliant, faultless,' said Alex. 'Actually, I prefer Benjamin and Belinda's. But I think Tammy and Charlie have got the edge when it comes to the actual skating.'

'Yes, but they haven't got Benjamin and Belinda's emotion, have they?' said Samantha. 'I tell you what I did learn; her name's really Tammy Mancuso.'

'She changed it to dance?' said Alex, surprised.

'Mm, Charlie Varker and Tammy Mann,' Samantha mused, then added, Samantha Stephens and Alex—?'

'Don't even think of it,' said Alex. 'Uh, oh, look who's here.' He nodded with his head. Belinda Thomas was threading her way through the cars towards them.

'Hello,' said Alex uncertainly, as she stopped in front of them.

'Don't let us keep you,' said Samantha.

Belinda smiled. 'I wanted a word with you,' she said.

'How about "Goodbye"?' said Samantha. 'That's a good word.'

'Leave it out, Samantha,' said Alex. He turned to Belinda. 'We didn't realize you'd be here.'

'Didn't you?' She smiled again. 'You must be the only people in the place who didn't, then. Charlie and Tammy stuck a greetings card to the windscreen of our car.'

'Where's Benjamin?' asked Alex.

'Oh, he's probably asleep somewhere,' she said offhandedly. 'Listen, there's something I think you should know. Well, more Samantha than you Alex.'

Samantha heaved a sigh but didn't speak.

'You can listen to me or not,' said Belinda. 'It's about your free leg – you're not always extending it when you dance the compulsories.'

'What?' said Samantha, very coldly.

'Not all the time,' said Belinda. 'Only occasionally, and only slightly, but it's a serious fault at the level you're skating now.'

'You've got the cheek to give me advice?' demanded Samantha. 'You seriously think I'm going to listen to you?'

'Well, no, but I thought I'd give it a try,' said Belinda. 'You see, it needs quite a time to put it right – believe me, I know. It took me over a year.' She gazed at Samantha's expression, then shrugged. 'Oh, never mind.' She turned away.

'Belinda.' Alex stopped her.

70

'Yes?'

'Charlie Varker didn't mention it when he skated with her,' he said.

'Well, he wouldn't be able to see it from where he was,' said Belinda.

'Walt didn't mention it either,' said Samantha.

'No,' said Belinda. 'He didn't, did he?'

11

KISSING ON ICE

'Again,' said Morris. Benjamin sighed and wearily let himself drift back to where Belinda was standing in the middle of the ice.

'And don't sigh!' snapped Morris. 'You really think I want to be here at this time of night?'

'Sorry, Morris,' said Benjamin. 'It's just, well, we must have done this bloody dance a hundred times tonight already!'

'Yes, you'd think you'd be getting it right by this time wouldn't you?' said Morris. 'Perhaps after another hundred times you will be.'

'Can we get on?' said Belinda. 'I mean, if McEnroe here has finished his little tantrum?'

Benjamin said something very rude under his breath, but like the professional he was, he took her in his arms and they went into their starting positions. They circled the ice a couple of times and when they started to talk it was on the far side of the ice, away from Morris, so there were long gaps in their conversation.

'You know, sometimes I wish I'd stuck to figure skating,' he said.

'And you think that's not repetitive?' demanded Belinda. 'All those dreary figures – besides, you were no good at it!'

'I could do a triple.'

'So could I.'

'Once! Once you landed a triple.'

'Yes, before I came to my senses,' she said.

'I bet you I still could.'

'Be serious, Benjamin,' she said. They skirted the end of the rink and she gave him a shake. 'You don't go risking injury! Especially not just before a competition – yes?'

'Yes, *sir*,' he said bleakly. They didn't talk for a whole circuit, cross with one another, and they stood in silence while Morris rewound the tape and started them off again.

'What did she say when you told her?' Benjamin asked at last.

'Who?'

'Samantha Stephens.'

'Oh,' she said. 'You knew then?'

'Be serious,' he said. 'I bet she was really keen to listen to you.'

'Well, half and half. She didn't want to listen but she couldn't stop herself.'

'I thought you always wanted to win?'

'I do, Benjamin,' she said seriously. 'But not at any cost.'

'It must be hell having to be so perfect all the time,' he said.

'We have Morris to help us, they haven't!' she snapped. He didn't answer and when she sneaked a look at him he was grinning broadly.

'You just shut up!' she said. They were silent again for another circuit but this time it was a friendly silence. The music ended and they let their momentum take them back towards Morris.

'Anyway,' she muttered, 'lots of people have helped us. We wouldn't have got this far if they hadn't!'

'I know.' Benjamin put his arm around her and kissed her cheek. 'Listen, sweetheart, if you hadn't told her I would have.'

Samantha sat on the kitchen table swinging her legs, watching her mother put tea together. Mrs Stephens was crashing dishes about. Samantha knew she was cross about something but hadn't found out what just yet.

'You got on all right with Walt, didn't you?' she asked. Mrs Stephens turned and gave her daughter a serious look.

'I think the less said about that episode, the better, don't you?' Samantha regarded her swinging feet for a moment. So it wasn't the car journey that was still upsetting her mother.

'As a matter of fact, your father and I both think Walt talks a lot of sense,' said her mother, after a minute.

'Why? Did he say he was going back to America, or something?'

'He said that you don't need to train nearly as much as you used to,' said her mother. 'We got the impression that he doesn't know exactly how much you do train.'

'Of course he does,' said Samantha, a bit too quickly.

'What do Alex's parents think about his skating this much?' asked Mrs Stephens.

'They're fine. *They* understand just how important it is.'

'Hm, perhaps I ought to have a word with them,' said Mrs Stephens, giving her daughter another look. 'Or, better still, I could talk to Alex this afternoon.'

There was a long silence before Samantha attempted to steer the conversation into safer areas.

'You were a model, weren't you?' Samantha said.

'Yes, not a very successful one, but, yes, I was a model,' said Mrs Stephens.

'Well, could you show me how to put make-up on? I mean properly, professionally.'

'Why?' her mother demanded. 'What do you want to go tarting yourself up for?'

'For the ice,' said Samantha, surprised at the reaction. 'Both Belinda Thomas and Tammy Mann make me look like a school girl.'

'You are a school girl,' her mother supplied.

'Yes, but I don't want to look like one when I skate in the British championships,' said Samantha. She studied her mother for a moment and then trailed a hook out:

'You do like Alex, don't you?'

'I do, I like Alex very much. So does your father,' said Mrs Stephens. 'He's a very nice boy. In some ways too nice for you, Samantha. You push him around too much. You push everybody around!'

'Oh, he needs it.' Samantha sighed, tired of this old conversation.

'Nobody needs pushing around!' said her mother. 'Does he like pâté?'

75

'Yeah, just give him anything,' said Samantha. 'I'll ring up and cancel him if that's what you want.' She was half hoping her mother would say yes, now.

'Don't say yeah, darling,' said her mother automatically. 'I don't mind him coming to tea at all, you know that.' Mrs Stephens put the big bowl of salad down on the table and stood looking at her daughter for a long moment.

'Look I . . . that is, your father and I, we don't mind you using the video recorder, but why does it have to be in your bedroom?'

Suddenly everything became clear to Samantha. 'Oh, Mummy.' She grinned. 'Look, it's got to be somewhere where we can watch it in private. You'll be in the sitting room, and Daddy, and we'll be watching the same moves again and again – and we have to be able to talk.'

'Hm – and they're just skating videos, are they?'

'Of course, what do you think they are? Video nasties?'

'No, of course not,' said her mother. 'And you say Liz got them for you?'

'Yes, Walt didn't seem to think it was a good idea,' said Samantha. She reached forward and took her mother's hand. 'That's all we'll be doing – honestly.'

Mrs Stephens studied her daughter again. 'You're not getting too fond of this boy, are you darling?'

'What does that mean? Too fond?'

'You know very well what it means.'

Samantha was quiet for a long moment, then she sighed. 'He's my skating partner. I'm sorry if this sounds hurtful but he's the most important person in my life – of course I'm *too* fond of him,' she said. 'But, if you mean are we sleeping together, then the answer's no.'

'Good.' Her mother gave her a hug. 'I'm sorry, darling, I had to ask.'

'That's all right – anyway, if I got pregnant it'd muck up my training, wouldn't it?'

Her mother tried to look disapproving but started to laugh instead. They were both still laughing when Mr Stephens and Alex came in together, but they couldn't tell them why.

An hour later Alex was lying on the floor on his stomach side by side with Samantha. Tea had gone very well. When asked about the amount of skating he was supposed to be doing with Samantha, Alex had backed her up all along the line. Mr Stephens had believed him absolutely. Alex had been so convincing that Mrs Stephens half believed him as well.

They were both watching a video of their free dance, Cloak and Dagger.

'I told you,' said Samantha, 'there's nothing wrong with my free leg at all.'

'We might not be able to see it on your television,' said Alex. 'Perhaps if we played it on the big one downstairs?'

'It'd still look exactly the same,' said Samantha. 'She's having us on.'

'But what's she got to gain from it?' demanded Alex. 'Besides, I don't believe she'd do anything like that.'

'Ah, it's just 'cos she's nice looking!'

'Oh, don't be daft.' Alex sighed. Cloak and Dagger came to an end and Alex replaced it with one of Benjamin and Belinda. They watched in silence for a few moments.

''Course she's attractive,' he said. 'She's amazing! But that's not the reason. I don't believe she'd play a trick like that. I suppose it's just possible she was trying to put you off but, I mean, they can hardly see us as competition.'

'Not yet,' said Samantha.

'Hang on a sec,' said Alex. 'She said on one of our compulsory dances. She didn't say on our free, nor on all our compulsories – that could be why no one else has noticed.'

'What? Even Walt?' demanded Samantha.

'I must be hearing things – you called him Walt,' said Alex. Samantha was frowning at being caught out.

'OK, if it'll keep you happy, we'll get someone to look for us,' she said.

'I'll ask Sue,' said Alex. His eyes were still fixed on the television. 'I wonder how much they train?' he said, half to himself.

'They train through the night, seven nights a week, and most afternoons as well,' supplied Samantha.

'How do you know?'

'I read an article on them last year in *Rink Link*,' said Samantha. 'I've still got it somewhere. I'll show you later.'

'But, what I really mean is do they train as long as we do each session?' said Alex. 'We're doing nearly four hours a night, Monday and Wednesday – you can't really imagine Benjamin training that much can you?'

She shrugged. 'I don't know, they were a bit cagey about that in the interview – so was Benjamin when we spoke to him in Bristol. Remember?'

'I didn't notice,' said Alex. Samantha was watching him closely, knowing he was still wondering whether she was right about their not training enough.

He pointed to the television. 'Look at that turn, there!'

78

He flipped the remote control and played the sequence again. 'See how she gets her balance from him. He doesn't put his arm around her waist as part of the dance but to stop her going over backwards – that's why it doesn't work when we try it.' They watched Benjamin and Belinda again and again before switching to Melodie Saxon and Lester Carmichael winning the National championships. Finally they played their own Cloak and Dagger free dance again.

After the tenth run-through Alex turned over on his back and gazed at the ceiling.

'Well, what do you think? You're the dance expert,' he said. She sat on the bed in case her mother came in. She had already dropped in once, 'to see if they were all right'!

'Benjamin and Belinda are so far ahead of us, they're on another planet,' she said. 'But we're better than Melodie Saxon and Lester Carmichael.'

'Are we?'

'Sure – I nearly went to sleep during their free.'

'Yes, but would we have got better marks from the judges?'

'You mean for Cloak and Dagger?'

'Yeah, you'll admit that theirs is technically better?'

Samantha shrugged. She hated admitting anything like that. Alex turned back to the television and they played their free dance once again.

'What do you think?' Samantha asked.

'I think we'd score better – just,' said Alex.

'So do I,' she said. 'If we'd been eligible for the Nationals, we'd have beaten them.'

'Not then we wouldn't, our compulsories weren't in the same league.'

'Now they are,' said Samantha. There was a long pause. They both lay there thinking. Then she said quietly:

'I'll tell you what though – Cloak and Dagger might well have beaten them a year ago, but this thing we're putting together with Wart wouldn't have.'

12

INTRUDER!

At two o'clock in the morning Birmingham Ice Rink stood cold and empty. Except, that is, for the two skaters who were standing on the ice, right at the edge.

Belinda shivered. 'Creepy.'

'What is?' Benjamin asked. 'This place? You should be well used to it by now – we spend more time here than we do at home!'

'No, I mean being watched secretly, like that,' she said. 'Good job you spotted him.'

'It's not creepy at all, just some idiot.'

'Some idiot with a video camera,' said Belinda.

'It's his video camera that gave him away,' said Benjamin. 'I saw the lens flash when Morris put on the main lights.'

'Don't you think you should go and see if Morris is all right?'

'Morris? Listen sweetheart, I'd rather have a Rottweiler coming after me than Morris in a bad mood – it's the bloke with the video camera I feel sorry for,' said

Benjamin. 'Anyway, he's got a security guard with him and I didn't think it was worth taking my skates off.'

'Well, I still think you ought to—' Belinda broke off as Morris came stomping down the aisle towards them.

'The security guard's got him,' he grunted. 'They're calling the police now.'

'How did he get in?' Benjamin asked.

'He's been hiding somewhere since the rink closed,' said Morris.

'Just so long as he's gone,' said Belinda.

'Yes, but what's worrying me is how he knew you were going through your new free dance tonight,' said Morris. 'Have either of you two been talking?'

'Oh, come on, Morris, we're not kids any more,' said Benjamin crossly, while Belinda just sighed and stared at the ceiling in exasperation.

'Well, somebody's talked, haven't they?' said Morris.

'Might have been a coincidence,' offered Benjamin.

'I don't believe in coincidences,' grunted Morris. 'There are too many people who'd like a preview of your new free dance, the press as well as other skaters.'

'Shall we get on with it?' said Belinda. 'I mean, I'd like to get some sleep sometime and I've got lectures all day tomorrow.'

'Yeah, and it's only a couple of months to the championships,' said Benjamin. 'Have you got hold of a list of entrants yet?'

'Of course,' said Morris.

'I thought it was strictly confidential?' said Belinda.

'It is,' said Morris. Then, to stop any more questions,

'No one you really need to worry about. Your main competitors are Anna Orlando and Steve Baker, of course.'

Belinda shrugged. 'We've beaten them the last three times,' she said.

'Don't you get too complacent, my girl. They're both good working skaters. You should win, but you can't afford any mistakes,' said Morris sternly. 'Then there's Melodie Saxon and Lester Carmichael.'

This time Belinda pretended to spit. Benjamin put an affectionate arm round her.

'Isn't she sweet?' he said, laughing.

'Go boil your head!' she snapped, shaking his hand off. 'You like them as much as I do, Benjamin Trueman!'

'Oh, yeah, they're about as foul as a box of frogs,' he said. 'They're not really serious competition though, are they, Morris?'

'They're improving all the time,' said Morris. 'Their compulsories are very good but I've no idea what their free dance is like.'

'Where do they skate?' asked Benjamin.

'Over at Basingstoke,' said Morris.

'Why?' asked Belinda. 'I thought they both lived in London?'

'It's so they can take the whole rink,' said Morris. 'I spoke to Colin, the rink manager – he's an old mate of mine. They have the entire place for at least two hours every day – they even get them to open up on a Sunday night.'

'That's why you don't know what their free dance is like,' said Benjamin.

'It makes you sick,' fumed Belinda. 'We're the British champions and we have to skate through the night to keep ours private.'

'It's that idiot father of Lester Carmichael's, he'd find any money to help his darling son,' said Morris. 'It was probably him who paid that bloke tonight with the video camera.'

'Bound to be,' said Belinda.

'You're going over the top, both of you,' said Benjamin. 'Just because you don't like them, you're imagining all kinds of things.'

'Maybe,' Morris nodded. 'The only other couple who seem to know what they're doing are Alex Barnes and Samantha Stephens.'

'Oh, yes, the ones I met the other week,' said Benjamin. He turned to Belinda. 'Have you spoken to them yet?'

'No, I have not! And I'm not about to,' said Belinda sternly. Benjamin grinned at her. Morris didn't notice.

'Keep it that way!' he grunted. 'They'll be competition one day.'

'It doesn't do any harm to talk to them,' said Benjamin. 'You talk to other skaters all the time – I've seen you giving them advice at competitions.'

'I have not,' said Morris. 'I am only too aware of the harsh realities of this business!'

'Ooh, Morris!' said Belinda, 'what about that couple in the Nationals, three years ago? You practically rewrote their free dance for them!'

'Nonsense!' said Morris crossly. He looked round for something to change the subject and said thankfully: 'Oh, good, here she is now.' A little old lady with piercing eyes was marching down the aisle towards them. Mrs Telford, the choreographer, had arrived.

'Oh, great!' Belinda grabbed Benjamin's hand and almost dragged him off into the middle of the ice. 'We'll just get warmed up,' she muttered.

Mrs Telford was a very severe woman, even more so at two o'clock in the morning.

'This is a ludicrous time to be out,' she snapped at Morris.

'I know, I'm sorry, Mrs Telford,' said Morris. Mrs Telford was just about the only person in the world he handled with kid gloves. He went on. 'You see, they always introduce their new free dance at the British championships, it's become a kind of tradition. This is the only time we can practise in private.'

'Absolute nonsense!' she snapped. Then she tapped the dancing stick she always seemed to be carrying. 'Come on, come on, let's get on with it!'

Benjamin came gliding across and handed Morris a cassette. Belinda stayed firmly in the middle of the ice. It was between competitions and she was slightly over-weight, and Mrs Telford was most unlikely to be polite about it. Morris slid the tape into his big dance cassette player and almost at once it found the beginning and started playing. Benjamin and Belinda went with it, letting it take them around the ice, fitting the separate moves, they had been working on for months, to the music. The record was long and the dancing ran out before the music did. The two skaters glided back to the side to hear the verdict. Automatically, they all turned first to Mrs Telford.

'How long did you say you'd got?' she demanded, 'before the British championships?'

'Er, two months, Mrs Telford,' supplied Morris.

'You are joking, of course!' she snapped. 'Tell me, have you two done any practice since I last saw you?'

'Yes, Mrs Telford,' said Benjamin, knowing better than to protest.

'Hm, too much messing about, as usual.' Mrs Telford prodded Belinda familiarly with her stick. 'Getting enough to eat, are we, dear?'

'It's this dress!' said Belinda crossly, as she always did.

'Well, it's a good thing. At least when you fall over you have plenty to fall on.' Belinda took a deep breath to control her temper. Mrs Telford was the best choreographer available and they couldn't afford to lose her.

'I have no intention of falling over,' she said slowly, 'and I'll take this weight off before the championships!' Benjamin tried to interrupt:

'What did you think of the music, Morris?' he asked.

'I'm not sure,' said Morris. 'The music's fine, but will it work without the lyrics?'

'I think so,' said Benjamin. 'Everyone will recognize it, anyway, and people know the words.'

'Maybe,' mused Morris. 'What do you think, Belinda?'

'If Benjamin says the music will work, it'll work,' she said, immediately.

'Wow! Is this really the Belinda we all know and love, talking?' said Benjamin, surprised.

'He's got a gift for it,' said Belinda, ignoring him. 'It's too long, of course.'

'Yes, how long is it, dear?' asked Mrs Telford.

'The original record's exactly six minutes,' said Benjamin. 'We'll have to lose the last two minutes, that's all.'

'Lose the last two minutes?' said Mrs Telford in a horrified voice. 'Don't be stupid, boy!'

'We've got to, the free's only four minutes long,' protested Benjamin.

'Thank you. I did know that,' she said. 'Lose two minutes indeed! I presume you are going to dance a love story again – yes?'

'Yes, Mrs Telford,' said Benjamin.

'Well, whoever heard of a love story without an ending?' said Mrs Telford. 'We need a whole record, beginning, middle, end, the lot!'

'How do we do that?' demanded Belinda.

'You'll have to have one specially recorded, that's all,' said Mrs Telford. There was a silence then Benjamin turned to Morris:

'Can we do that?' he asked.

'Oh, yes,' said Morris. He pulled a face. 'The main problem is money. Are you really stuck on this particular record?'

'Yeah, we are,' said Benjamin. 'Sorry.'

'No, don't be, it's better you feel that way about it,' said Morris. He sighed. 'I suppose I'll have to go shopping for cash again.'

'Can we get on?' said Mrs Telford. 'I don't want to waste my time.'

'Yes, you'd better make it work, if we're going to go to all this trouble,' said Morris.

'Oh, it'll work,' said Mrs Telford. 'They'll make it work.'

'Eh? Thank you, Mrs Telford,' said Belinda, surprised.

'It'll be reasonably easy for them,' said Mrs Telford.

'You mean, because . . . well, that we can skate OK?' said Benjamin.

'No, because it's a love story,' she said. There was a silence while they all looked at her. It was most unusual for Mrs Telford to praise anybody or anything. She heaved a sigh of exasperation at their baffled looks. 'Well, you're in love aren't you?' she demanded. 'That's why it works on the ice. It comes across, the crowd senses it.'

Belinda had gone bright red, Morris was grinning and Benjamin had decided his skates needed adjusting.

'Well, come on,' snapped Mrs Telford. 'Anyone can fall in love, dears, that's easy. Now, showing it by dancing, that's the tricky bit.'

13

SINGLE MINDED

Sue and Liz stood watching intently as Alex and Samantha skirted the end of the rink.

'Dammit, you're right,' said Liz. 'I can't believe I haven't spotted it before.'

'It's only for a couple of seconds,' said Sue.

'That's hardly an excuse!' Liz beckoned Alex and Samantha over and they broke off their dance and came shooting across, worried expressions on their faces.

'You were right,' said Liz. 'It's only on the turn and during the blues, but it's right under the judges' eyes – they'll spot it a mile off.'

'Hell!' said Alex. Samantha said something a lot ruder.

'A beginner's mistake!' she snapped. 'How could it happen, Liz? I mean, have I always been doing it?'

'No, it's just something you've slipped into,' said Liz. 'It's probably from skating on the small rink over at the Coliseum. I've seen it before – you get worried about hitting the barriers with your free leg and subconsciously you bend it out of the way.' Liz looked unhappy. 'I'm sorry, I should have noticed it.' Alex immediately came to her defence.

'It's not your fault, Liz,' he said. 'You haven't been working with us on the compulsories, just lately.'

'No, it's Wart's fault!' said Samantha, savagely.

'It's easy enough to miss,' said Sue. 'He never stands at the end of the rink, anyway.'

'Well, he should!' said Samantha. 'It's supposed to be his job!'

'Look, it doesn't really matter whose fault it is,' said Liz. 'The important thing is, we've found out early enough to correct it.'

'It's a bad habit to get out of though, isn't it, Liz?' said Alex, worried.

'Normally, it's a swine,' said Liz, 'but Samantha's an ex-dancer. Now she's aware of it, she'll soon get it right.'

'I'm going to get it right tonight,' said Samantha, bitterly. 'Dumb amateur's mistake!'

Liz glanced around at her dance class which she had left at the other end of the rink. 'I'll stay afterwards and work with you.'

'Thanks, Liz,' said Alex.

'It's a good job you spotted it,' said Liz. 'It would have cost you half a mark at least – that's a couple of places at your level.'

'We didn't spot it,' said Alex. 'It was Belinda Thomas.'

'Belinda?' said Liz.

'She only did it to gloat,' said Samantha. 'She's a cow!'

Liz smiled. 'I take it you've only met her at competitions?' she said. 'She's not a cow at all. She's just a bit single minded – like someone else not a million miles away.'

Samantha still didn't want to believe it, but she nodded grudgingly and dragged Alex off across the ice.

'You sure you don't mind working a bit late tonight?' she said. 'You're not rushing off to a football match or anything?'

'That's a highly intelligent remark, isn't it?' he asked. Samantha was silent for a moment.

'Yes, you're right – I'm sorry,' she said, uncharacteristically. 'I'm just a bit fed up about this leg business.'

'I know.' He gave her arm a squeeze in one of his rare shows of affection. 'Don't worry, we won't leave here until we've got it right.'

'Now, are we sure it's just on that one compulsory?' said Samantha.

'Well, we'll run through the lot just to make sure,' said Alex. 'I can see it, now I know what I'm looking for. Then we can concentrate on the bits that matter.'

'Thanks, Alex,' she said quietly.

'That's all right, I want a favour anyway,' he said. 'I need you to cover for me.'

'OK,' she said, immediately.

'I've told my parents that I'm staying over at your house on Thursday night. I've said your dad's running us to the Basingstoke rink early on Friday morning. If they say anything . . .' His voice trailed away.

'You want me to lie – yes?'

'Well, yes.'

'OK,' she said.

'I didn't think you'd mind – you're a good liar.'

'Hm,' she said. 'Any chance of you telling me where you're going?'

'I'm going with Toby to a late night football match,' he said, very casually. 'I didn't think they'd be mad keen.'

'Right.' She held out her arms to him and they took up their stance. Their eyes met.

'I do mind lying to them, Alex, but of course I will, for you,' she said. 'And I am a good liar' – she gave him a look – 'better than you are!' He avoided her eyes and they started to skate.

On Thursday afternoon Toby was sitting, gazing sadly at a tureen of soup. The double doors to the kitchen crashed open and a beaming Alex strode in. Over the other side of the kitchen, Martin started angrily at the noise but relaxed when he saw who it was.

Toby looked his friend up and down, then he returned his gaze to the soup. He sighed.

'I'm glad you're pleased to see me,' said Alex.

'What?' Toby glared at him. 'I wouldn't be particularly pleased to see Escoffier at the moment.'

'Doesn't he play for Manchester United?' said Alex.

Toby frowned. 'What do you want?'

'Twenty quid,' said Alex. He flinched away, waiting for the explosion. Toby reached into his jacket pocket, produced a tatty wallet, and handed over a twenty pound note. Amazed, Alex held it between finger and thumb as though it were red hot.

'Toby,' he said worriedly, 'are you all right?'

'Oh, I'm fabulous,' said Toby. 'All day I've been working on that' – he pointed – 'I spent hours on the stock alone! I chose the finest vegetables, the very best spices, the freshest cream, the most expensive olive oil in the world! I laboured over it, stirring it gently for hour after hour. I watched it like a cat, and, and'— Toby broke off, lost for words. He gulped to regain control – 'and I turn my back for five seconds and it goes and boils on me!'

'Boils? So what?'

'Alex, it's boiled! It's a soup, not a lobster.'

'Does it matter?' said Alex. He stuck a finger into the tureen and licked it. 'Tastes fine to me.'

'Don't let me keep you,' said Toby bleakly.

Alex grinned. 'Don't you want to know what I need the twenty quid for?'

'There are other things in life than money,' said Toby. He regarded the dish in front of him again and added sadly, 'Soup for instance.'

'Ah, open a tin,' said Alex. Then, at his friend's infuriated gaze, he held up a hand. 'OK, OK, I'm off. Thanks for the loan.'

Toby returned to his reverie. Alex wandered over to where Martin was working. Martin avoided his gaze. Alex placed an arm around his shoulders and gave him a friendly hug.

'Mate!' he said affectionately. Martin looked even more worried. Alex winked and blew him a kiss, then exited, still clutching his twenty pound note.

The music died away in the darkened rink leaving the couple in an embrace that was so close it seemed like their bodies were almost one. The girl gazed adoringly into the

93

boy's eyes long after the dance had finished. At last they reluctantly parted and even then she kept hold of his arm as though she couldn't bear not to be touching him. The emotion was so strong between the couple, it crackled through the deserted building. At last, the girl shook herself out of her stupor and the perfect lips of ice dancing's most beautiful asset spoke:

'You airhead!' said Belinda.

'OK, so I made a mistake – it happens,' said Benjamin.

'Made a mistake! You went the wrong way!' Belinda stormed. 'At one point I thought I was going to have to lift you!'

'I suppose you never make mistakes?'

'Not ones we can't cover up, I don't.'

'What about when you fell over during that competition in Birmingham?' Benjamin asked.

'What about when you left your skates on the train?' Belinda demanded. 'Or managed to lose your locker key ten minutes before we went on?'

Benjamin regarded her for a long moment. 'At least I've never eaten so much that my new costume had to have the waist let out the night before a medal test,' he said softly.

'Ooh,' Belinda thrilled, 'you rat! You absolute rat! You promised never to mention that again!'

'Oy!' came Morris's shout. The two skaters came back to earth and let themselves drift over to him.

'Have you stopped arguing now?' he demanded.

'We weren't arguing, Morris,' said Benjamin. 'Just having a little discussion.'

'Yeah – the argument comes later,' said Belinda. She

gave his arm a punch. 'You just wait!' Benjamin grinned, but didn't answer. He turned to Morris:

'What did you think of it?'

'The ending was perfect,' he said. 'Perhaps you should just go right into that.'

'The whole middle section doesn't work,' said Benjamin. 'It doesn't feel right.'

'No, I think we should be together, touching, the whole time,' said Belinda. 'That is the theme of the record, after all.'

Morris sighed. 'It's getting a bit close to do any radical changes.'

Benjamin shook his head. 'It doesn't work, Morris,' he said. 'I'd rather do our old free than this, the way it is now.'

'OK. Have you any ideas?'

'Yeah, I want, I want' – he broke off, then – 'I want to make the audience cry.'

Belinda was about to make a wisecrack, but the intense look on Benjamin's face told her it wasn't the moment. The three of them always created their free dances between them, but Benjamin was always the one who added the emotion.

'The ending's right. The beginning's fine,' said Benjamin. 'Now all we've got to do is to keep the middle section in exactly the same mood – we don't need all the flashy stuff, not for this record.'

'You're right,' said Belinda. 'And I think I should stop turning my back on you, we should be looking at each other for virtually the whole dance.'

'That's it!' said Benjamin excitedly. 'A bit like that Russian couple, Oksana Gritschuk and Evgeny Platov. It shouldn't be too hard to adapt our free.'

'No.' Morris sighed. 'After all, it only means changing everything.'

'Ah, come on, we'll soon get it right,' said Benjamin.

'Oh, yes, dead easy!' said Morris sarcastically. He glanced at his watch. 'You'll have to give me a minute. I'll have to phone Louise.'

'What for?' demanded Benjamin.

'Because she's well used to me working until five, but she gets a bit worried if I don't come home at all.' He made his way up the aisle. 'She always thought I was barmy, but that was until I met you two.'

Benjamin looked at Belinda. 'Is it really that late?' he asked.

'Yes.'

'Oh,' he said wonderingly. 'Well, another couple of hours should see us through.'

'Yes. Then all we've got to do is to resurface the ice,' said Belinda. 'And then lectures start at nine.'

'Lectures?' said Benjamin. 'Oh! What day is it?'

'Well, it's Friday now,' said Belinda. 'After all, we've only been going three hours. We can't be tired yet!'

'Tired?' said Benjamin. He glanced around the empty stretch of ice and a grin spread across his face. Before she knew what he was doing, he'd taken off like a speed skater, rocketing around the rink. He circled twice before leaping high in the air and executing the most perfect triple of his life, landing only feet away from Belinda. He bowed.

'Told you,' he said, bigheadedly. She stared at him as though in admiration.

'Flash sod!' she said.

It was seven-thirty before the two exhausted skaters and their weary coach stepped out into the cold morning air. And the figure who had been huddled behind the rubbish skips was jerked awake at the sight of them. Alex Barnes, who had thought he had missed them, watched in amazement as they collapsed into Morris's car. He stayed hidden as they drove away and gave his watch a last wondering look. Then he gave himself a shake and jogged off towards the railway station to catch his early morning train.

14

TOGETHER
ON ICE

Alex lay on his bed staring at the ceiling. It was Sunday morning and he was trying to enjoy the luxury of a lie-in, like he used to do every Sunday before Samantha had started dragging him out for a run. Three months ago Walt had told him to quit running and a delighted Alex had been only too happy to agree. Samantha hadn't said anything, just nodded.

He stretched and pretended he was enjoying himself, thinking how this made up for his lost night's sleep on Thursday. But somehow it wasn't nearly as good as he had been imagining, all those mornings when Samantha had bullied him up the hills. The door opened and his mother came in carrying a tray with a mug of tea and some toast on it. She didn't mind waiting on him at all. She was only too pleased that he wasn't training as much of late. Neither of Alex's parents liked or understood ice dancing, and the way it always came before everything else worried them.

'A letter came for you, yesterday,' she said putting the tray down. 'From Birmingham.'

'Birmingham?' He sat up and took it. 'Thanks, Mom,'

98

he said, taking a sip from his tea. She stood watching him from the door as he ripped the letter open and read it.

'Who's it from?' she asked.

'Oh . . . um, a bloke called Morris,' said Alex. 'He's Benjamin Trueman's and Belinda Thomas's trainer.'

'What's he writing to you for?'

'Er . . . he's just wishing us luck in the British championships,' said Alex, deliberately casual.

'That's nice of him,' said his mother.

'Yeah,' said Alex. When his mother had gone he lay back in his bed gazing at the celing.

Samantha ran most days but Sunday was her big run because, apart from an evening of skating practice, it was her day off. Her circuit covered seven miles and two big hills. She sped along, her feet hardly seeming to touch the ground, enjoying the feeling of her body working well. She turned the corner and suddenly Alex was running at her side, pace for pace. They ran in silence for a couple of minutes before he spoke.

'Did you get a letter?'

'Yep.'

'Oh!' The first hill approached and they dug deeper trying to keep the same pace. It began to hurt. Samantha was pushing herself. Now, it was no longer just a stroll. A hundred metres before the top Alex broke and fell behind. Samantha didn't falter, just kept pushing until at last she reached the brow of the hill.

'Ow, hang on a sec,' Alex gasped from behind. She paused, still jogging on the spot, watching the perspiring figure battle up to her.

'Hell,' he panted. 'You'll have to give me a bit of time.'

'I won't give you a single day,' she said quietly, and turned her back on him.

'Samantha!' His voice was almost plaintive and Samantha, in spite of herself, had to turn back.

'Come on,' he said. 'I'll soon get back into it.' She was glaring at him, then, at last, she stopped running and waited for him to draw level.

'You've cost us three months,' she said in a low, furious voice. 'Three months! Because you listened to someone else rather than me – damn you, Alex Barnes!'

'He's our trainer!'

'And I'm your partner! You of all people should know what that means – only another skater can understand. How could you put someone else before me?'

'Look, I'm sorry.'

'I don't want your apologies.'

'Well, what do you want, Samantha?' he asked. 'Do you want to find a new partner?'

'Don't be so stupid!' She shook her head in exasperation and reached up and pushed him hard in the chest. 'You really want to know what I want, Alex?'

'Tell me.'

'I want an Olympic gold medal!' Her voice was quieter now, but her eyes were burning with intensity. 'Not a silver, not a bronze, not a European or a British championship – I want an Olympic gold medal! And if I have to work every day of my life for the next ten or twenty years, that's what I'm going to get! Now do you understand?'

He nodded. 'I've always understood.'

'Well, then, I'll tell you something else: I need you for that. What's even more important, I want you! I want you there holding my hand when we get presented with it,' she said. 'So, don't you ever, *ever*, let me down again!'

'OK.' He put his hands on her shoulders. 'I want to be there too, Samantha, holding *your* hand. Now, I've said I was wrong, you were right. I should've believed more in you. Just give me a bit of time to put it right, that's what partners do for each other, isn't it?'

She studied him for a long moment, and at last gave a nod. 'Yes, that's what they do,' she said. 'I tell you what, it takes three days to get unfit and three weeks to get fit again, yes?'

'So they say.'

'Well, you've got three weeks.'

She turned and took off down the other side of the hill and this time Alex was right alongside.

Toby opened the door of Alex's bedroom and went inside. Alex was face down on the carpet doing push-ups, or trying to. He took a deep breath and pushed hard, his arms shuddering, as inch by inch he forced his body up off the floor.

'One hundred and fifty,' he gasped and collapsed. Toby sat on the bed, swung his legs up, produced a Mars bar and contentedly started to eat it.

'One hundred and fifty, eh?' he said, conversationally. 'Pretty impressive.'

'I used to do two hundred every day – one hundred of those straight off.'

'Ah, well, you just live for pleasure,' said Toby, lying back. 'Are you ready or have you forgotten we've got a pool match arranged?'

'I can't come – sorry,' said Alex. He rolled over onto his back and started doing a series of sit-ups, his body moving like a metronome. Toby didn't seem at all put out by this information.

'I knew your heart wasn't in it,' he said easily. 'Back to full time training, are we?' There was no answer but the gasps from Alex's protesting lungs.

'I wondered how long it would be before she brought you to heel,' said Toby. Alex paused for a second and gave his friend a dangerous look.

'It has nothing to do with Samantha,' he said coldly.

'No, 'course it hasn't,' said Toby. 'Actually, I don't mind staying in this evening. There's this Chinese cookery programme on Channel 4.'

'I'll try not to miss it,' said Alex. 'Ah! One hundred!' he gasped and took another rest. He regarded his friend soberly. 'I should get an early night if I were you,' he said.

'Why? What's this sudden concern for my health?' Toby demanded, suspiciously.

'That's not fair, Toby – you know I'm always worried about you.'

'And?'

'Well, I need a favour.'

'Oh, no.'

'You got your motorbike yet?'

'Yeah, picked it up today,' said Toby enthusiastically. 'Do you want to see it?'

'Why? It's a motorbike, isn't it?' said Alex absently. 'Just so long as it goes.'

'Oh, it goes,' said Toby with a grin. 'What does this favour entail?'

'You might have to get up a bit early.'

'No way, pal!' said Toby, definitely. 'I'm off getting up early for life. Anyway, I thought you'd given up your paper round – you know, the one I used to do for you?'

'Not all the time you didn't, just occasionally,' said Alex. He lay back on the carpet and started doing leg lifts. 'It's only a small favour.'

'It doesn't involve money, does it?' Toby demanded. 'I haven't had my twenty quid back yet.'

Alex avoided this. 'I just need you to come to the Coliseum, tomorrow morning sometime.'

'Oh, is that all?' Toby relaxed. 'Any specific time?'

'No – doesn't matter,' said Alex. 'Long as it's before seven.'

'Seven o'clock, that means getting up at six,' exploded Toby, coming to his feet.

'A bit earlier, I would have thought,' said Alex. 'It's important you're not late.'

'No way, pal,' Toby repeated. 'Nothing on earth will get me out of bed before six o'clock in the morning.'

Alex grinned, then went back to his exercises.

15

TRIPLE JUMP

The sports doctor lifted Belinda's leg up from the couch.

'Hurt?' she asked. Belinda shook her head vigorously.

'Young lady, if I'm going to help you at all, I need you to tell me exactly what you feel,' the doctor said. 'Now, does that hurt?'

'A bit,' Belinda admitted. The doctor put her leg back down again and sighed. She glanced over at Morris and Benjamin who were standing, watching anxiously.

'When does she have to skate on that knee again?' she asked.

'This afternoon,' supplied Morris. The doctor frowned, then prodded Belinda's knee with one finger. She wasn't a particularly sympathetic woman and Belinda had to bite her lip to stop herself crying.

'How did she do it?' the doctor asked.

'By being a stupid idiot!' said Belinda, and now she was crying.

'She did a triple jump, missed her landing, and went into the barriers,' said Morris.

'It was my fault,' muttered Benjamin.

The doctor turned to him in surprise. 'How so?'

'Because we don't do triples in ice dance,' he said. 'Only, I had to, didn't I? And Belinda copied me.'

'Hm, she's a big girl,' said Morris. 'She's responsible for her own actions – what's the damage, doctor?'

'See, here.' The doctor beckoned them forward and pointed. 'The swelling's nothing, it's just the haematoma – a blood clot underneath the skin. That will go down within the week, but she's pulled the ligaments holding the knee joint in place.'

'What does that mean?' demanded Morris. 'Is it serious?'

'It's knee damage – all knee damage is serious,' said the doctor. She shrugged. 'Three weeks to start to repair, three months before it's better – if you're lucky.'

'Yes, but can she skate on it?' Benjamin asked the million dollar question.

'Strap it up tightly – she can skate on it this afternoon,' said the doctor. 'But it's going to hurt!'

'I can skate,' said Belinda from the couch.

'Isn't there anything you can give her?' Morris asked.

'A bullet to bite on?' said the doctor. She raised her eyebrows as though waiting for a laugh but, not surprisingly, nobody found her particularly amusing.

'I was thinking more in the way of pain killers,' said Morris.

'Aspirin – don't take too many,' said the doctor. 'I can give her something a bit stronger but she'll have to stop taking them well before this competition or a drug test will pick it up.'

'Is there nothing you can do?' demanded Benjamin, annoyed at her off-hand attitude.

'Physiotherapy might help – it increases the blood supply to the damaged tissues, and strengthens the muscles.' The doctor considered Belinda's knee again. 'Trouble is though, the blood supply is already good to the knee and the muscles are just about as strong as they can get . . . it could help a bit. If you go that route, you'll need a session every day, and you'll not get it on the National Health.'

The doctor picked up a pad and scribbled on it. She ripped off the prescription and handed it to Morris.

'No more than three a day, and remember what I said about drug tests.'

'Right then, doctor,' said Morris. 'Thank you for your help.' Morris tried to help Belinda off the couch, but she pushed him away and limped instead.

The car journey back across Birmingham was spent in a heavy silence: Benjamin was still annoyed at the doctor, Morris was annoyed at both Benjamin and Belinda, and Belinda was annoyed at everybody in the whole world. Morris parked the car in a bus stop, outside a chemist. He half-turned in his seat to look at Belinda who was lying on the back seat, her leg out straight.

'This isn't the time to tell me off,' she warned.

Morris shrugged. 'I have no intention of telling you off,' he said. 'You've got to expect injury. You've both been exceptionally lucky up to now.'

'Yeah, but it was the fool way I did it,' said Belinda savagely. She pounded on the back of his seat with her fist. 'Damn! Damn! Damn!'

106

'It was my fault,' said Benjamin.

'It doesn't matter, does it?' said Morris. 'Just learn by it.'

'That doctor wasn't exactly nice, was she?' demanded Benjamin.

'She's one of the best in the country,' said Morris. 'She damn well ought to be, the prices she charges – that cost thirty-five pounds.'

'Thirty-five pounds?' Benjamin's voice rose. 'We were only in there for ten minutes! And she didn't do anything.'

'You're not paying for what she does, but what she knows,' said Morris.

'I said we should have gone to my doctor,' said Belinda. 'He's lovely – and he's free!'

'And all he would do is tell you to have three months off. He might even have immobilized your knee,' said Morris. 'Sports doctors are not just specialists in sports injuries, their job is to get you back into training as soon as possible.'

'Yeah – I guess,' said Belinda, still not totally convinced.

A bus came up behind the car. The driver leaned out and shouted angrily at them, but Morris ignored him.

'We can just about afford thirty-five pounds,' said Morris. 'That's not the issue. What we have to decide is what we do now.'

'How do you mean?' Benjamin asked.

'He means, do we drop out of the British championships?' said Belinda. 'And the answer is no!'

Morris smiled. 'Well, that is one of the options, yes. But I do know you fairly well after all this time,' he said. 'No, I mean, do we plump for the physiotherapist?'

107

'Every little helps,' said Benjamin. 'How much does it hurt, Belinda? I mean really, no messing about?'

'It hurts like hell,' she admitted.

'OK, then. These are your options,' said Morris. 'The best physiotherapist I know costs twenty pounds a session. That's one hundred and forty pounds a week for eight weeks – say a thousand pounds if I can cut a deal.'

'Ow,' said Benjamin.

'The thirty-five pounds tonight just about wipes out the last of the sponsor's money,' said Morris. 'You've got nothing, and you won't get anything more until – and if – you win the British championships again. Benjamin's dad won't help, and you won't ask your parents for any more money, Belinda – is that right?'

'Absolutely,' said Benjamin, not Belinda. 'They've helped enough.'

'Fair enough, I can understand that,' said Morris. 'Now, the session this Saturday is costing two thousand pounds, which we've already budgeted for. I can probably still cancel and get most of the money back which would give us enough for the physio, and some over to ease the way.'

There was a long silence, broken only by the angry revving of the bus as it pulled out round Morris's car. There came a blast from the bus's horn. Nobody in the car even noticed.

'What it comes down to in real terms,' went on Morris, 'is this: is Saturday worth two thousand pounds? Or, to put it more bluntly, is Saturday worth more than all the pain you're going to go through?' He opened the door. 'I'll go and get your tablets, Belinda. You two talk about it, let me know what you decide.'

Benjamin sat back in his seat, put his feet up on the dashboard, and closed his eyes. After a moment he said:

'Thirty-five pounds for ten minutes. I think I'm in the wrong business.' He yawned. 'And she didn't even give you a sweet.'

'Eh?' Belinda said, still occupied with her thoughts.

'My doctor always used to give me a sweet,' said Benjamin.

'Ah, but did your doctor have her wonderful bedside manner?' said Belinda.

Benjamin grinned. There was a long silence before Belinda spoke again:

'We're supposed to be talking it over,' she said. 'Morris wants our decision when he comes back.'

Benjamin didn't even open his eyes. He grinned. 'Do you want to talk it over?' he asked.

'Don't be silly,' she said.

On Saturday morning, at eleven o'clock, Benjamin and Belinda were standing in an attic, in the middle of London. It was a big attic and it was fitted out as a recording studio, but it was still an attic. There were a dozen musicians fussing around with their instruments, playing short tuneless bursts and trailing wires up and down in search of electric sockets.

Self-consciously, Benjamin and Belinda stood inside a soundproof office with the music editor while the musicians played the whole piece over and over again. At

109

twelve o'clock, everybody broke for lunch, which arrived in the form of coffee and sandwiches, before getting on to the real work of the day. Each of the musicians recorded their own piece separately, some of them sounding most odd with long pauses between short snatches of seemingly disjointed notes. Benjamin and Belinda couldn't make out how they managed to get their timing exactly right, but the editor pointed out the earphones they were wearing through which a piece from the morning session was being played in its entirety. Some of them had to play their sections again and again before the editor was satisfied; the saxophonist at one point threatened to walk out, before he was pacified. The editor kept asking Benjamin and Belinda whether the various instruments were producing the music they wanted, but they couldn't tell and wisely left it to the professional.

It was four o'clock before it all came together. The musicians went home and the editor started mixing the various recordings to produce the final piece of music. The first mix he tried sounded wonderful and it got better as he endlessly varied the mix and volumes of the instruments, warning Benjamin and Belinda how it must sound for a packed ice rink.

It was seven o'clock before they were issued with a tape each of the end product. It was ten-thirty before they arrived back, at New Street Station, in Birmingham, and Morris was waiting. He drove them straight back to the rink and by eleven-thirty they were skating on the empty ice to the final version of their music. For weeks now they had been skating to a track which included vocals, and that wasn't allowed under ISU rules.

110

It was after three in the morning before they got to bed. They were lucky, it was Sunday which meant they didn't have to be on the ice again until four o'clock that afternoon.

16

COUNTDOWN TO COMPETITION

SATURDAY:

'So I told her straight,' said Alex. 'Mrs Kennedy, I said, I'm skating two sessions a day until Saturday and there's no way I can hand in any homework until after the weekend.'

'Now, this bit,' said Samantha, hanging on to him so their turn was very tight, his leg just missing the barrier. 'See, we've got the whole run of the ice for the bob.'

'Hey, that's not bad,' said Alex. They stopped and viewed the mass of skaters packing the ice. He gave her a nudge. 'Let's go for it,' he said. 'Might injure a few beginners but sacrifices have to be made.' She grinned at him and they skated carefully through the circle of struggling beginners around the bar.

'So, what did she say? Mrs Kennedy, that is,' Samantha asked.

'Oh, she said that I was an illiterate reprobate, and, whereas that didn't matter in the natural order of things, she wasn't having anybody saying that, after two years of her teaching, she had turned an illiterate reprobate loose on the general public. She also said that if I didn't do the work she'd report me to the Head Teacher, that she'd get me suspended, that she'd write to my parents and she'd do her utmost to prevent me taking the exam next year.'

'Oh,' said Samantha. 'She took it better than you expected then?'

'Yeah,' grinned Alex. 'I guess I'm lucky she's a skating fan.'

SUNDAY:

Morris came stomping down the aisle. Benjamin and Belinda, who were on the ice, heard rather than saw him because all the lights had gone off right in the middle of their free dance. They could tell from Morris's walk that he was annoyed. A torch clicked on and now they could just make him out. In the middle of the rink it was slightly brighter, the ice gleaming eerily in the moonlight that came flooding through the skylights.

'It isn't a fuse,' said Morris. 'The whole blasted town is off!' He was almost dancing with rage. 'If it isn't one thing, it's another: power cuts, knee injuries, idiots with video cameras.'

'Oh, yeah, did you find out what happened to him?' asked Benjamin, to get off the subject of Belinda's knee.

'The police had to let him go,' said Morris.

'Why didn't they charge him?' demanded Belinda.

'What for? Important though your free dance might be, it's hardly a breach of the Offical Secrets Act to video it!'

'What about breaking and entering?' said Benjamin.

'But he didn't. He just stayed behind in one of the toilets – no law against that,' said Morris.

'So, there is no way we can find out who sent him?' said Belinda.

'At this moment I don't much care,' said Morris. 'I'm more concerned with the ice melting, now the electricity's gone off.'

'Have you rung anybody?' Benjamin asked.

'Who do you want me to ring? Bird's Eye?' Morris demanded.

'The Electricity Board?' Belinda offered.

'I'm sure somebody there knows,' said Morris. 'It's not going to make them work any faster, me moaning at them.'

'It makes us work faster when you moan at us,' said Benjamin. 'Well, it's cost us a night's practice.'

'Don't be ridiculous!' snapped Morris. 'The cassette player's battery powered, you can see the edges, you can see the ice – get on with it!' He pressed the button on the cassette player and the music boomed out. Taken by surprise Benjamin grabbed hold of Belinda and they raced off after the music. They circled the ice once, then, when they were out of sight on the far side, she gave him her grin.

'Told you,' she said. 'That's a quid you owe me.'

MONDAY:

Walt blew his whistle and Alex and Samantha let the momentum from their dance take them to the edge.

'I think we're getting somewhere at last,' said Walt. 'Your compulsories are really quite good now.'

'Thanks, Walt,' said Alex. 'They felt right, didn't they Samantha?' Samantha gazed at Walt and nodded.

114

'Well, we've got one more session on Thursday morning,' said Walt. 'We'll go through the entire programme then.'

'Aren't we doing anything on Friday?' Alex asked.

'Oh, no, have some time off. You don't want to get tired out for the big day,' said Walt. 'I don't want you even looking at the ice from Thursday morning until the compulsory practice on Saturday.'

'Yes, Walt,' said Alex. Samantha gave him another one of her nods.

'It's just about the end of the session,' said Walt, as ever glancing at his watch. 'Now, remember what I said, don't go tiring yourself out this week.'

'Absolutely,' said Alex. Both the skaters slid guards onto the blades of their skates and walked with him up the rubber steps to the changing rooms.

'See you on Thursday then, Walt,' said Alex, at the door.

'Yes, OK, Alex, Samantha,' he nodded to them, and hurried off up the corridor. They watched him until he was right out of sight then they turned and made their way back down onto the ice.

TUESDAY:

'So, you keep to the basic turn,' Morris said over his shoulder. 'You heard what Mrs Telford said: it's more than adequate for the British championships, no sense in taking risks and it'll be less hard on your knee, Belinda. We'll have nearly a whole year to get the new turn right for the Olympics!'

He drove the car through the gates under the sign that

115

read: 'University of Birmingham', and parked by the barrier across the road.

'What do you think?' he asked, when there was no response. He turned around. Benjamin and Belinda were leaning against each other in the back seat, fast asleep.

WEDNESDAY:

Alex froze the video and pointed to the screen.

'See, look there. Your leg's absolutely straight.'

'Yes, it's not bad,' said Samantha. 'Let's see it at the other end of the ice – go on a bit.' Alex pressed the slow advance button on the remote control and they watched the video closely as though they hadn't seen it twenty times already that night.

It was late, and they were in Samantha's bedroom, lying on the carpet, watching themselves on video. Samantha's mother was patrolling the landing. She had already been in twice. They had been skating all evening and Liz Pope had videoed their compulsories during her dance class.

The video came to an end and they both turned over and gazed at the ceiling.

'It looks a bit better,' said Samantha, grudgingly.

'It looks damned good,' said Alex. 'You did OK in the time you had.'

'You didn't do so badly yourself,' said Samantha. 'You beat my three week deadline easily, didn't you?' He was saved from having to find an answer because there came a tap on the door and Toby walked in.

'Am I interrupting something?' he said with a grin.

'No, you are not interrupting something!' said Samantha, very loudly, in case her mother was still outside.

116

'What do you want, Toby?' demanded Alex.

'I've found out what you wanted,' he said.

'Oh, it's about time,' Alex grunted. 'It's taken you long enough.'

'You ungrateful sod. I've had to get up twice a week at some unholy hour—'

'Yes, Toby,' interrupted Samantha. 'Don't listen to him, we're very grateful.'

'Yes, we're very grateful,' said Alex flatly. 'Now what did you find out?'

'It's just as you said,' said Toby, sitting down on Samantha's bed.

'Ah.' Samantha gave Alex a significant nod.

'Well, it doesn't exactly come as a surprise,' said Alex. 'But it's nice to have some proof. Cheers, Toby!'

'Don't go over the top now,' said Toby. 'I don't trust you when you're being nice.'

'Toby,' said Samantha slowly, 'I bet you don't know what Britain's first colony was.'

'Eh?' said Toby, baffled at the question. 'Bermuda, wasn't it?'

'Oh,' said Samantha, disappointed.

Toby shook his head. 'Well, if there's nothing else you want me for, I'm going to catch up on some sleep,' he said, getting to his feet. He went and opened the door.

'Hey, you are coming on Sunday, aren't you, Toby?' Alex called after him.

'Of course I am,' said Toby indignantly. 'I'm putting a hamper together. I've heard the food at Nottingham Ice Rink isn't up to much.'

They heard him talking to Samantha's mother on the

landing. She was trying to keep her voice low. Alex sat up and gazed down at Samantha.

'I've been thinking,' he said.

'Good,' she said, patronizingly.

'It is you,' he said.

'It is me, what?' she said, surprised.

'It's you who's been taking my shoes all this time, isn't it?' Her wide-eyed innocent look told him he was right.

'I must've been blind,' he said, trying to sound cross.

'I thought you'd never catch on.' Samantha was laughing.

'Have you still got them?'

'Of course,' she said. 'I was going to start putting them back, one at a time, after this weekend.'

'Why?' he demanded. 'Why did you do it?'

'Well . . . you were getting on my nerves,' she said.

'You get on my nerves as well,' he said, lying back down again. There was silence for a minute, then he added quietly, 'Not all the time, though.'

THURSDAY:

Benjamin, dressed in a tracksuit, was drinking coffee in the Students' Union. He was leaning against the counter talking to a pretty girl with very blonde hair.

'Push off, Debbie!' came Belinda's voice.

'Charming, I'm sure,' said Debbie, turning to find Belinda glaring at her. 'I was only—'

'Don't bother,' said Belinda. 'Look, just go and dye your hair or something.' The girl shrugged, gave Benjamin a quick smile, and disappeared into the mass of students.

'You're in a good mood,' said Benjamin.

'I'm having some problems with one of my lecturers,' she said.

'Yes, I can see that's a good reason for having a go at Debbie,' said Benjamin. 'She was only being friendly.'

'I know what she's being!'

'She's in my maths set,' said Benjamin, grinning. 'And you know how keen I've always been on figures.'

'If you want me to clear off so you can talk to her, just say the word.'

Benjamin nodded sagely. 'OK,' he said. This time he was really laughing. He reached out and touched her forehead. 'My word, you are getting overheated, aren't you?'

'Don't you patronize me, Benjamin Trueman,' she said crossly. He didn't answer, just kept on drinking his coffee and smiling at her. After a moment she had to let a ghost of a smile loose.

'Oh, shut up!' she said.

'Which lecturer?' Benjamin asked.

'Mrs Hughes. She's moaning about a report I should have had in by last weekend.'

'Rosie?' demanded Benjamin. 'Not even you could fall out with Rosie!'

'You wouldn't like to bet on that?'

'Silly of me,' said Benjamin. He crushed the cup and dropped it into the waste bin. 'I'll have a word with her, give her a couple of tickets for Sunday – she'll be fine, don't panic.'

'Crawler,' she said.

'Yeah, I know,' he said. 'Come on, we've got twenty lengths of the pool to do for your knee.'

119

'I really ought to get that computer programme finished,' said Belinda. 'Else I'm going to upset Mr Stokes as well.'

'Yeah?'

'Yeah!'

'OK,' he said levelly, and turned and made for the door that led towards the swimming pool. Belinda watched him for a moment, then gave a shrug.

'Yeah,' she repeated, and followed on after him.

FRIDAY:

'What have we here?' said the police driver to his colleague, who was drinking a cup of tea from a flask.

'Looks a bit out of place, doesn't he?' said the second policeman as the figure in shorts and a T-shirt came running past the parked police car.

'I think we'd better have a word,' said the driver, starting up the engine. They cruised forward and drew up alongside the running figure. The second police constable wound down his window.

'Hold on a minute, son,' he said. The figure stopped but continued to jog on the spot.

'What's your name, son?'

'Alex Barnes.'

'And what are you doing out at two o'clock in the morning?'

'Five miles,' said Alex. 'I'm on a training run.'

'Don't you think it's a bit unusual to go running at this time of night?'

'It's the only time I've got free,' said Alex. The driver leaned across so he could get a better view.

'Wait a minute. I know you, don't I?' he said. 'You're that ice skater?'

'Ice dancer,' said Alex. 'How did you know?'

'My daughter skates over at the Coliseum,' he said. 'She's quite a fan of yours.'

'Oh – thanks,' said Alex.

'Yes, it's the British championships this weekend, isn't it?' said the driver. 'Tomorrow, in fact.' He glanced at his watch. 'Today.'

'Yeah. It's a practice in the morning, compulsories in the afternoon and the free dances on Sunday,' said Alex. 'Can I go now? I'm wearing the pavement out.'

The second policeman was still looking disapproving.

'Do your parents know you are out at this time of night?' he asked.

'No,' said Alex. 'I mean, I don't suppose they'd be exactly surprised, but they don't know.'

'So, what if we tell them?'

'There'd be a row! Dad'll shout, Mom will cry, then they'll forbid me to go out again at night,' said Alex. 'Then, next week I'll be out here just the same. It's the only time I've got free,' he said again. 'Can I go now?'

The driver smiled, in spite of himself. He started up the engine.

'You take care now,' he said. 'Best of luck this weekend, Alex.'

17

THE POWER
OF LOVE

Alex watched in admiration as Samantha eased her legs into the full side splits position. He was still amazed at her flexibility, a legacy from her ten years of dance training.

They were both very nervous. This was the biggest event so far in their lives. Other skaters were everywhere but nearly all of them had that preoccupied, quiet look that said: 'Leave me alone'. There was a large crowd waiting for them on this, the last day of the British championships. Somewhere out there were Samantha's parents, Toby, Liz and most of her dance class. And, for the first time, Alex's parents had come along.

The holders, Benjamin and Belinda, were in the ante-room with all the rest but protected from everybody by their ever-present watch-dog, Morris. Benjamin had smiled and waved hello to them but Belinda was studiously ignoring everybody.

'Look at them,' said Alex, a bit put out by Belinda's attitude. 'Just sitting there, all relaxed, knowing they've got it in the bag.'

'They might well have *this* competition in the bag but

they're still as frightened as we are,' said Samantha. 'They've got a lot more to lose.'

'Look.' Alex gave Samantha a nudge and she glanced across the room. Belinda had laid back on the bench, a cushion behind her head, her eyes closed. 'She looks dead worried,' said Alex, sarcastically. Samantha lowered her voice so she wouldn't be overheard:

'She was being sick in the toilets, ten minutes ago,' she said. This immediately got Alex on Belinda's side.

'Oh, was she? Sorry,' he said, though the person to whom he was apologizing was too far away to hear. 'They handle it better.'

'They've had more practice.' She eased her legs out of the splits position and rolled effortlessly to her feet.

'Alex,' she said. 'I want to ask you something.'

'If it's money you want, then, I'm sorry, you're out of luck.'

'No, seriously,' she said.

'Believe you me, I am being serious,' he said. 'I still owe Toby ten pounds!'

She ignored this. 'Am I too pushy?'

'Why?'

'Well,' she paused, then, 'I've had a letter from Monica.'

'The girl you train?'

'Used to,' said Samantha. 'It's a nice letter. She's written to thank me for all my help. But she says that she doesn't want to take any more medals, just wants to skate for fun. That she can't handle the intensity of training I expect from her.'

'Well, it gets you off the hook, doesn't it?' said Alex.

'Alex,' she said. 'Just answer the question, will you?'

123

He grinned. 'Yes.' He reached for her hand. 'You're the most pushy person I've ever met,' he said. 'But I need that. We wouldn't have made it half this far if you weren't that way.'

'It's just that to do something, half well, seems so . . . pointless,' she said.

'Yeah, I know that now,' said Alex. 'That was why Belinda was being sick in the toilets earlier.' Samantha squeezed his hand back. He glanced over her shoulder.

'We've got company,' he said, letting go of her hand. She looked up. Morris was stomping in their direction.

'Hi,' said Alex. Morris grunted a reply.

'Your compulsories have come on a lot,' he said. 'You deserve better than fourth place.'

'We thought so, too,' said Alex. He grinned. 'But, then again, we always do.'

'You've got to serve your time, get your name known – give the judges something to look for,' he said. 'That's how it works with ice dancing – Benjamin and Belinda had to learn that, too.'

'We know, Morris,' said Alex. 'Samantha here doesn't like it, but we can wait a bit.'

'But only a bit,' Samantha said quietly.

'Yes, but . . .' Morris broke off as a man with a camera slid through the door – one of the press who had slipped through the security net. Morris said one sharp sentence that was so rude it made even the hardened reporter blink. He slid out again looking sheepish. Morris went on as though nothing had happened. '. . . But you realize that today is when you start making your name?' he said.

'Yes, Morris, we realize that,' said Alex.

'Where is he?' Morris demanded.

'Walt? Oh, he's around. I expect he's out watching the skating,' said Alex.

'Who's on?'

'Melodie Saxon and Lester Carmichael,' supplied Samantha.

'Oh, yes, I see,' said Morris, turning away. 'Best of luck both of you,' he said over his shoulder.

'Morris,' said Alex. He turned back. 'We owe you.'

'Yes, you do.'

'Why?' demanded Samantha. 'Why did you help us?'

'For Ice Dance,' he said. 'For the beauty of it.' He shrugged. 'You'll understand one day.' He stomped away. There was a pause before Alex said, very quietly:

'I think I already do.' He looked at Samantha. 'You taught me.' He leaned forward and gave her a kiss, the first one for some weeks. She gave a watery smile.

'Now, don't go all soft on me,' she said.

Alex grinned. 'I think it's about time,' he said getting to his feet. They both put their skates on very carefully and made their way to the tunnel that led out onto the ice. They sat on the rubber floor very close together. They weren't on for some time yet but this was where they always sat, where they could hear the music of the other skaters, but not see the marks. And this was where a beaming Walt found them some five minutes later.

'Nearly time,' he said, rubbing his hands.

'How did they do?' asked Alex, levelly.

'Eh? Who?' said Walt.

'Your two of course: Melodie Saxon and Lester Carmichael,' said Samantha.

'What do you mean, my two?' he demanded.

'We know!' said Alex, getting to his feet and pulling Samantha up beside him.

'Know what?' Walt's smile had slipped an inch.

'About you being Melodie Saxon and Lester Carmichael's trainer,' said Alex. 'About Lester's father paying you to come over from America especially.'

'You see, we couldn't work it out,' said Samantha. 'We thought that NISA was paying you so I checked with Sir Robert Sinclair, but he said no. Then someone else in the skating world said they'd seen you training those two over at Basingstoke.'

'Oh, this is nonsense,' said Walt, still smiling.

'Is it?' said Alex. 'I thought we must be imagining it all, so I got a friend of mine to follow you on his motorbike. He's not very good, kept falling off, or losing you – he got booked by the police once, but he finally came through a couple of days ago.'

'He saw you training them for three whole hours,' said Samantha. Then she repeated softly, 'Three whole hours!'

'Well, what if I did? I help those two out sometimes – they pay me. I help you two out for free,' expostulated Walt.

'No, you don't. We were warned that you never do anything for free,' said Samantha. 'Lester Carmichael's father pays you to train us. Well, that's putting it badly. He pays you to make sure his precious son wins.'

'And that meant putting us out of the running,' said Alex. 'So you attacked our strength, our free dance! You totally knackered that up for us, didn't you, Walt? But you had to do something to justify your existence, so you

126

concentrated on our compulsories — and, you know what you did? You turned them into a strength as well!'

'Well, I'll say this, you certainly have an imagination,' said Walt. 'Why on earth would I bother with you? You're ranked below Melodie and Lester anyway. I'd go for Benjamin Trueman and Belinda Thomas.'

'Yes, but you'd never get past Morris,' said Samantha. 'I bet you had a try, didn't you? Morris mentioned something about a bloke with a video camera. Did you arrange that as well, Walt?'

'Oh, Morris — that's where all this is from,' said Walt. 'He's paranoid, that one.'

'Yeah, I rather think he is,' said Alex. 'Though he didn't actually accuse you of anything. Just mentioned he'd seen you over at Basingstoke, and then he added a couple of points that really made us think. He told us that, whatever happens, Anna Orlando and Steve Baker are retiring after this British championship, and also that only two couples from here are going to be picked for the Europeans — we just put two and two together.'

Walt didn't say anything, but now, for the first time since they had met him, his smile had disappeared completely. Samantha came close to him and looked right into his eyes.

'So, a third place here would guarantee them a place in the Europeans — and the only people that had any chance of getting in the way were us,' she said. 'A good showing, there, would almost certainly mean a place in the Olympics next year. Get their name known in time for the next one! What's his father trying to do, Walt? Buy him a medal? — oh, sorry.' She had brought the blade of her skate down with crunching force on the toe of his trainers. He gave a gasp of agony and slid down the wall, clutching his foot. Alex looked stunned at the sudden transformation. Tears of pain, outrage and shock were pouring down Walt's face.

'I believe that's us, Alex,' said Samantha.

'Eh?' said Alex, still mesmerized by the sight of Walt flopping around on the floor.

'The PA system has just read out our names,' said Samantha.

'Oh – right!' said Alex. Hurriedly they both stripped off their tracksuits, unzipping the trouser bottoms so they'd slide over their skates.

'They're already way ahead of you,' Walt gasped from the floor, through gritted teeth. 'You'll never make it up.'

'We'll see,' said Samantha. 'Don't run away!'

Callum Gardner from BBC Television picked up the microphone in the commentary box:

'And here we have the young couple lying in fourth place after the compulsories . . . two of our rising stars, Alex Barnes and Samantha Stephens . . . this is the first time they have appeared on television . . . their strength is said to be in the free dance . . . I actually saw their free dance this morning and it was capable and well skated but I wouldn't have said outstanding . . . apparently they thought the same, because they've requested a music change for the final . . . most unusual, that. I wonder if they've decided to skate an old free dance . . . we'll soon see . . . here they are, Alex Barnes and Samantha Stephens.'

Over the country, people glanced up at the tone of

Callum Gardner's voice, sensing something a bit different, and watched as Alex and Samantha skated to the centre of the ice.

'They're dressed absolutely the same, in a kind of ski suit . . . but the material's glittering white . . . very stunning.'

Samantha reached for Alex's hand and gave it her usual quick squeeze. They both took a deep breath because their dance had to start the instant the music started and the first sequence was very fast skating. They literally had to take off like arrows.

'These two don't hang about . . . oh, yes, their music is the theme music for the Winter Olympic Games . . . the speed they're skating is quite remarkable . . . both leaning forward like speed skaters . . . ah, yes, I see . . . they're parodying the Winter Olympics.'

Back on the ice the two skaters' speed slowed right down and their movements changed to the more exaggerated ones of skiing, first the long slow motions of cross-country skiing, then the wide sweeps of the slalom before picking up speed again for the downhill.

'Well, I don't know whether you can strictly call this ice dancing . . . these two are certainly slick and their entertainment value is . . . ah, now we're being treated to a bit of figure skating . . . and now, what's this . . .'

Alex came right up behind Samantha and she sank down into a crouch on her skates, her arms held out behind her as Alex pushed her along furiously like he was starting a bobsleigh, and now the crowd was cheering as the two skaters shot the entire length of the ice.

'These two can skate, can't they . . . she gets up again

with no trouble at all . . . and now . . .' Callum Gardner started to laugh.

And so did nearly everybody watching because Alex and Samantha were faced-off in the centre of the ice, chasing an imaginary ball as they pretended to play a game of ice hockey. They were coming to the end and the most risky part of the whole production; this was where they could offend the judges.

'And, at last, we're into the ice dance . . . that's a nice touch . . . they're a bit cheeky this couple . . . that sequence was from Benjamin Trueman and Belinda Thomas's free dance from last year's British championships . . . and that final move is pure Benjamin and Belinda.'

Alex was holding Samantha very close, but they didn't stay like that for the dramatic length of time that Benjamin and Belinda would have held the move, because the music changed and they immediately stood bolt upright for a short rendition of the National Anthem as they pretended to collect their medals.

'Well, well, well, that was a bit different . . . the crowd certainly liked it . . . they might not have a realistic chance of winning today but they've captured the hearts of everyone here . . . Benjamin and Belinda had better watch out . . . these two are snapping at their heels . . . they've certainly thrown down the gauntlet . . . they're a bit late for next year's Winter Olympics but there's no doubt that the intention is there . . . let's see if the judges have a sense of humour . . . here we go . . . oh, the marks are quite good . . . except for the ninth judge – that's very low . . . Peggy Willmot obviously likes her skating really serious . . . those were for technical merit, the next ones are for artistic impression . . . oh, those are even better . . . I think that should take them right up into second place behind Steve Baker and Anna Orlando with only Benjamin and Belinda left to skate . . . that should guarantee them third place in their first British championships.'

Alex and Samantha went back to the tunnel to hide. Walt had disappeared. They sat holding hands watching the two famous figures, whom everybody had come to see, out on the ice.

A hush fell as Benjamin and Belinda took up their stances in the very middle of the rink. The wait seemed to go on for ever before the first evocative notes of their music came echoing across the ice, taking them with it. From the very first bars, everyone recognized which piece they had chosen to dance to: 'The Power of Love' – the record made famous by Jennifer Rush. And it was all so obvious, so clear, so absolutely right for Benjamin and Belinda. Nobody spoke, nobody clapped. In the commentary box Callum Gardner was silent. Nobody existed in the whole rink but the two lonely figures out on the ice. Never taking their eyes off one another, never letting go, never even turning away, the emotion between them fizzed and crackled through the auditorium. The audience was held in a trance; afterwards they would swear that the two skaters had danced for an hour but, of course, it only lasted for four minutes. The fullest four minutes of their lives. At last the music faded away, but still the two skaters were locked into one. There was a stunned silence. Benjamin and Belinda had to break it, finally coming back to life and releasing the audience to applaud like they were never going to stop. Even then, Benjamin and Belinda didn't notice, their eyes still gazing into one another's as they glided out of the spell of their dance towards the edge.

Alex gave Samantha a nudge with his elbow.

'Are you crying?' he asked.

'Not really.' She wiped her eyes on her sleeve.

'Cheer up,' he said. 'Third place was what we came for.'

'I'm not upset, Alex. I know we couldn't win. All we were really after was a place in the Europeans.' She shivered. 'It's just that, well, they were pretty good, weren't they?'

'Brilliant.'

'You know why they can skate like that, don't you?'

'You tell me.'

'Because that's how they really feel about each other,' she said. She pulled his face down and kissed him. 'We will be able to skate like that one day, won't we, Alex?'

'You mean, as perfectly?' He was grinning at her.

She kissed him again. 'You know what I mean,' she said.

Nicholas Walker
Crackling Ice £2.99

'My name's Alex Barnes,' he said, but obviously she didn't care. There was a long silence. 'You're supposed to tell me your name now. That's how it works.'

She turned her eyes on him. 'Will it shut you up if I do?'

Dancing means everything to Samantha. But she is forced to leave dance college and go to a new school, where she meets 14-year-old Alex Barnes.

Samantha is skating against all the odds: her arch rival Diane, her parents' suspicions, Alex's reluctance to take competing seriously . . . will she ever skate to win?

A behind the scenes story of the glittering world of ice skating.

Nicholas Walker
Skating on the Edge   £2.99

Alex Barnes and Samantha Stephens sat on the floor just inside the
tunnel that led out on to the expanse of ice. Samantha was leaning
back against the wall, her eyes closed. She hugged herself and
shivered . . .

Samantha collapses on the ice right in the middle of a major
competition. Her parents send her away to boarding school and ban
her from ice skating – and Alex.

Can Samantha and Alex find a way to train in secret? Will Samantha's
new headmistress expel her? With the Junior Championships just
around the corner, time is running out . . . fast.

All Pan books are available at your local bookshop or newsagent or can be ordered direct from the publisher. Indicate the number of copies required and fill in the form below.

Send to: Pan C. S. Dept
            Macmillan Distribution Ltd
            Houndsmills Basingstoke RG21 2XS
or phone: 0256 29242, quoting title, author and Credit Card number.

Please enclose a remittance* to the value of the cover price plus: £1.00 for the first book plus 50p per copy for each additional book ordered.

*Payment may be made in sterling by UK personal cheque, postal order, sterling draft or international money order, made payable to Pan Books Ltd.

Alternatively by Barclaycard/Access/Amex/Diner

Card No.   ☐☐☐☐☐☐☐☐☐☐☐☐☐☐☐☐

Expiry date   ☐☐☐☐☐☐

. . . .
Signature:
Applicable only in the UK and BFPO addresses

While every effort is made to keep prices low. It is sometimes necessary to increase prices at short notice. Pan Books reserve the right to show on covers and charge new retail prices which may differ from those advertised in the text or elsewhere.

NAME AND ADDRESS IN BLOCK LETTERS PLEASE:

. . . .
Name . . . .
Address . . . .
. . . .
. . . .
. . . .